DRAGON MISSING

DRAGON MISSING
DRAGON APPARENT BOOK ONE

TALIA BECKETT

This book is a work of fiction. All of the characters, organizations, and events portrayed in this novel are either products of the author's imagination or are used fictitiously. Sometimes both.

Copyright © 2020-2022 Talia Beckett
Cover by Bandrei
Cover copyright © LMBPN Publishing

LMBPN Publishing supports the right to free expression and the value of copyright. The purpose of copyright is to encourage writers and artists to produce the creative works that enrich our culture.

The distribution of this book without permission is a theft of the author's intellectual property. If you would like permission to use material from the book (other than for review purposes), please contact support@lmbpn.com. Thank you for your support of the author's rights.

LMBPN Publishing
PMB 196, 2540 South Maryland Pkwy
Las Vegas, NV 89109

Version 1.10 November, 2022
eBook ISBN: 979-8-88541-663-4
Print ISBN: 979-8-88541-664-1

To Bryan. For showing me that I am worth more than I thought and believing in me since the humble days of Imperio and my first ever draft of that first book.

— Talia

THE DRAGON MISSING TEAM

Thanks to our Beta Team:
John Ashmore, Kelly O'Donnell, Rachel Beckford

Thanks to the JIT Team:

Zacc Pelter
Christopher Gilliard
Dorothy Lloyd
Deb Mader
Wendy L Bonell
Diane L. Smith
Jackey Hankard-Brodie
Angel LaVey
Paul Westman

If I've missed anyone, please let me know!

CHAPTER ONE

All I could hear was the slow *drip-drip* of the kitchen faucet through the slightly open apartment door. And that scared me more than anything. Not that it was dripping—it had done that for years—but that it was the only noise. Anthony, my sort-of mentor, was always up to something.

Taking a deep breath, I squared my shoulders and raised my head, imagining his words.

Scarlet, posture is everything. If you want to appear calm and confident, you have to position your body in a calm and confident way. Put your head up, lift that chin. Show people you know who you are.

That was all well and good for him. He knew who he was. An eccentric handyman who lived in the bottom apartment of my building and spent the rest of the time writing journalistic papers on bizarre insects from South America.

I was just the girl who lived in the trust fund apartment several floors up, by myself. Before you ask, that didn't make me a rich kid. I had no idea who had left me the trust fund, and it wasn't much. It covered my rent and a few bills. I worked in a tourist café on the beach to pay the rest of the bills and save up for college.

It wasn't going so well.

I did my best. I worked hard. Anthony wouldn't cut me any slack. However, life was expensive in LA. And I only got so many hours of work. Sometimes the tips were good, but more often, they weren't.

Wondering why Anthony hadn't fixed his leaky faucet when I knew he was capable of it, I knocked on his door again. It wasn't like him to leave me waiting, and silence wasn't like him either.

After a few seconds, I hmphed and tried the door handle. It wasn't locked, and it swung open. It was never locked. Anthony liked an open house.

"It's me," I said, no other words following. I'd intended to make a wisecrack about the faucet, but I stopped as soon as I saw the main room.

Anthony's belongings were strewn everywhere, cupboards tipped out, and contents scattered. All the insect jars had been broken, and their occupants were crawling or jumping here and there or otherwise long gone. There was no sign of my friend.

I froze, terror gripping my heart and squeezing tight. This didn't happen to normal people. This was like a scene on TV.

"Anthony?" I called and took another couple of steps, being careful not to step on a beetle. There was no reply.

Fear settled into my body, like a weight in my stomach and pressure in my chest. Bunching my hands into fists, I moved forward, making my way closer to the kitchen and the dripping tap.

I called my friend's name a couple of times, but there was nothing but the drip and the strange chirp of some insect from near the back wall. This wasn't good. Not one bit.

Not sure what else to do, I checked all of the rooms, from the living room to the kitchen, then to the bedroom and the small guest room he used as an office.

They were all in the same state—his belongings were scattered everywhere. I didn't want to step on the debris or look at it too closely. Anthony was a private person, and though I was worried about him, this felt like an invasion of his privacy.

After I'd checked every room twice, I stopped. With no idea where he'd gone and a mess that made it look as if someone else had been looking for him, I had no idea what to do.

I'd seen cop shows where people went missing or came home to find it looking like this, but having it actually happen? I didn't know what to do. The shows skipped ahead to the cops being there. Did that mean I needed to call them? Would Anthony want me to?

I didn't know. Looking around the living room once more for anything that might answer any of my questions, I realized his laptop was gone. Could he have taken it with him?

All sorts of theories ran through my head as I walked aimlessly through the apartment again. I didn't know what I expected, but I looked for anything that might offer up information.

Torn about respecting his privacy and getting some clue as to his whereabouts, I stooped to examine some papers that had been pulled out of a desk drawer.

They were bills and had been neatly filed away, little labels sticking up on tabs. I flipped through them until I saw a folder that said "Cotton Candy."

Tilting my head to the side, I looked to see if anything was in it. Anthony had called me "Cotton Candy" ever since the day we'd met. I'd shown up at my apartment with no keys and no idea of how to do anything. I'd been eighteen, fresh out of high school, and more than happy to get out of state care.

He'd found me sitting on my suitcase outside the door of the apartment after an hour of knocking and trying to get hold of someone who might know how I was meant to get in, all with no response. All I'd had with me was a big tub of cotton candy, my goodbye present from another kid.

But why did Anthony have a folder with those words on it? I knew I wasn't supposed to touch anything, so I hooked the edge of my sleeve over my finger and thumb and used it to lift the flap on the divider.

Although it looked as if it had once contained enough to weigh this divider down and crease it, there was nothing in there now except a few photos of me. One was of Anthony and me, but it had been ripped and I was no longer in it.

Not sure what that might mean, but curious, I removed the photos and shoved them into my pocket. Either Anthony had taken the rest of the contents or someone else had. It seemed important, and that was good enough for me.

I straightened and was trying to decide if I should keep going or call the cops when I heard a noise from the front door.

"Ant?" Mrs. Jenkins called in her high-pitched voice. "I can't get the..."

I stepped into the living room as she came through the front door, and her voice trailed off as she looked around. Her shock equaled mine when I'd found the place.

"What on earth happened?" she asked, her voice somehow going up another octave.

"I...don't know. I only got here a moment ago. He's not here."

"Oh, you poor thing. This isn't the kind of thing a young 'un like you should see." She opened her arms, clearly intending to hug me.

My body went to her automatically. I'd spent enough years being passed around foster homes where everyone wanted to welcome you as if you were part of their family and hug you whether you liked it or not, that I knew it was better to get it over with.

She did just that, ushering me out of the building as she embraced me.

"Stay here. I'll call the police, and we'll let them sort it out." She pulled out her cell phone, the kind with an extra-large font and a huge and clunky case.

I watched her struggle to open it and figure out how to dial the numbers, even considered offering to do it for her since the wait was almost painful, but I knew it wouldn't help. Mrs. Jenkins liked to mother people. She especially liked to mother me.

Eventually, she got the police on the phone and gave

them the building address and a brief explanation of what we'd found. By brief, I mean she told them how dreadful it was, how devastating and that a young girl shouldn't have been the first to find it. The male voice on the other end eventually cut her off and told her someone was on the way but it might take half an hour because it didn't sound like we were in any direct danger.

Mrs. Jenkins didn't think this was good enough and sucked in a large breath to say something along those lines, but the dispatcher hung up.

That left her with no one but me to talk to.

There was an awkward pause while she tried to decide whether I needed mothering or if she could complain more. If I hadn't also been confused and worried, I might have tried to look more upset so she would stick with mothering me.

"Some people really shouldn't be in jobs like that," she said, her chins wobbling as she lifted them higher.

She sucked in another breath, confirming my fear that I would have to listen to her whine about the cops these days and how awful this was for her.

"Here's us, finding such a horrible thing. No idea if the handyman is even alive. No one to fix the problems in our houses, and they want to make us wait half an hour for someone to even come and look. I'm not young anymore. You shouldn't be exposed to such a thing, and I shouldn't be on my feet for so long. My ankles. I'm not young anymore. I was saying to June only yesterday how..."

I zoned out, not sure I wanted to listen and unable to think about anything beyond finding a file labeled with my nickname that had photos of me in it. That didn't make sense. I wasn't special. I barely even needed Anthony to do much these days. I'd paid attention to him as he'd fixed things for a year, and I'd learned to fix them myself.

Now I mostly talked to him to hear someone's voice. We also played board games and cards. He liked to play games, and I didn't mind it either.

Anthony had different board games. Not like Monopoly or Risk or the cheap, tacky games based on books or movies when they were popular. He had the ones that made you think. Obscure expensive ones with lots of pieces and long rule books.

They were the kind of games you could play for hours and not grow bored, and we did. It was the best way to spend a Saturday evening.

Not that I was a geek, or a nerd. I liked to party and drink, and I took care of my hair and makeup. You didn't survive the other girls in the foster homes if you didn't look and sound like you fit in. I didn't have to do that with Anthony, though. He didn't care.

"And the poor little fluff ball. He'll be meowing for me already." Mrs. Jenkins paused to take another breath.

"Maybe you should go back to him," I said, sensing my moment.

"And leave you here with this horrible mess? You'll be scarred for life."

"I'm much calmer now. Knowing the cops are on the way is a big help. I can stay here. Mr. Leroy really shouldn't be left alone. You know he can get himself in such awful scrapes when you're not there."

"He does, doesn't he? He's such a silly little cat. Are you

sure you'll be fine? You still look pale." She squinted as she studied me as if checking I was still the same color.

"I've been indoors a lot lately. It'll do me good to be out here in the sun."

That did the trick. Mrs. Jenkins nodded, thought about her cat, and made her way back toward her apartment on the other side of the building.

I exhaled as I watched her go. At first, I felt better, able to think without her chatter, but then I noticed how quiet it was again. And that Anthony wasn't here.

I didn't do panic. There wasn't much point. It wasted time and energy and didn't achieve anything, but this strange, numb, lack of surety was the closest I came to it. I wasn't bothered by most things. I was no stranger to hunger or thirst, and I didn't know what it was to feel safe. Most people who made threats had no follow-through, and those who did knew what they wanted and generally made their expectations clear.

There was nothing to panic about.

Now, however, I wondered if it might help. I had feelings I didn't know what to do with. I was worried. I liked Anthony, and I couldn't say that about many people. He'd *never* not been there. Not since the first day, when he'd found me a key to my apartment and gotten the power on for me.

I didn't need him now the way I'd needed him then, but I wanted him. And the more the minutes ticked by, the more I was sure he wasn't coming back. At least not right away.

It left me with one painful realization: I was on my own. Again.

CHAPTER TWO

By the time the cops arrived, I was yawning, and my feet ached. I'd also wrapped my arms around myself. I was getting cold in my t-shirt; the sun was going down and the light no longer reached the courtyard in the middle of the apartment block.

The cops hadn't turned up in half an hour. It had been more like an hour and a half before two of them waddled through the parking lot, looking left and right until they spotted me.

"You the girl that found the trashed apartment?" the thin one asked. He was balding and had combed what was left of his hair over the top. That was the hairstyle I understood the least. Why did people try to hide what couldn't be hidden?

I didn't speak but tilted my head down and up before turning to the open door. They didn't let me get more than a few meters before the younger cop reached out to stop me.

"Best if you don't go inside. Wouldn't want you to find something you shouldn't see or disturb the evidence."

"I've already been inside," I said. "I was looking for Anthony. Door wasn't even open. And I normally get takeout with him on Thursdays."

The officer looked down at me, finally paying me some attention. I waited, knowing there was no point rushing the cop's appraisal. He would decide if I was okay or not and nothing I said would make any difference.

"Anthony lives here?" he asked a moment later. He took a step back and pulled out a small notepad.

"Yes. He's the handyman for the apartments and he has been kind to me. I live alone in one of the other apartments, and I come down to have takeout and play board games with him on Thursday evenings."

"So, the two of you are dating?"

"No! He's ancient, and—"

I stopped talking when the cop looked at me as if he didn't believe me. How could we have been dating? Neither of us got within a meter of the other most of the time. Anthony had never so much as hugged me or held out an arm to guide me except in a few rare circumstances where I'd closed the gap. Now that I thought about it, I'd never seen him initiate any kind of physical contact with anyone.

And there hadn't ever been a girlfriend over the four years either. He'd just been Anthony, the handyman. Anthony, the stable guy with respect for all living creatures. Anthony, the researcher of interesting games and provider of problems to solve. Anthony, the constant presence.

"He's more like an uncle," I said a moment later, sure it was the worst thing to say the second I'd finished saying it.

The cop raised an eyebrow and carried on jotting. I frowned. This wasn't right and it was getting far, far worse.

"Can you find him?" I asked, hoping I could distract him.

"That will depend on what's in there, but often, when this sort of thing happens, the person doesn't want to be found."

The cop was trying to let me down gently, but they didn't know what I did. Anthony wasn't the sort of guy to just give up on. He also wasn't the sort of guy to just leave without saying goodbye. Something had happened to him.

Some*one* had happened to his apartment.

The officer asked more questions to find out what I knew. Thankfully, as we talked and the longer it went on the more the cop figured out that nothing was happening between us.

Over the course of our conversation it became apparent I'd already been in the apartment, and it continued to get darker outside, so the cops let me stand just inside the door while they investigated further.

"His laptop is gone," I told them as I watched Comb-Over go toward the second bedroom.

"You know that for sure?" the other one asked.

"Yes. He didn't use it like normal people use their laptops. It never left the desk."

"So we might have a thief."

"Nothing else is missing that's valuable," I replied, although I felt like I shouldn't have to.

Both cops frowned at me and made me wish I hadn't

spoken. I guess they didn't like being told a difficult truth or that they were thinking about this wrong.

I watched them a little longer and saw one of them flinch when a cricket jumped near him.

"What's with all the bugs? Did the guy not have pest control?"

"He collected them. Wrote about them. That was his other job. I think. On top of being everyone's handyman."

Young Cop grimaced and paid more attention to where he stepped. Most of the insects were long gone, though. I felt a pang of sadness creep into my heart. The collection had been something he was proud of and now it was gone, and it probably hadn't been his choice.

I wasn't sure exactly what it had meant to him, but it would have meant something to him and so its destruction bothered me. I wasn't used to that feeling either.

"I can't find anything to identify this guy," Comb-Over said. "No passport. No driver's license. No photos."

"I could describe him," I replied, hoping to be helpful. It would be awful if they couldn't find him.

"That only partially helps, but you seem to know him better than anyone else here, and we've got no alternate contact yet. I think we need to have a bit of a chat. Why don't you tell us his details like his surname and if he has family or other friends. Anyone we might be able to talk to, to get an idea of who might have done this?"

"You think someone targeted him?" I asked as I moved to the nearby footstool and perched on the edge. It was one of the few things that wasn't covered in debris.

"Can't be sure yet, but it's not very likely, given what you've told us. More likely to be a burglary, and Anthony will walk through the door at any moment without a care in the world."

"At least until he sees this," Comb-Over added.

It wasn't funny to me but Young Cop laughed as if he found it so before taking a look at the shelves full of board games. They had also been tipped out all over the floor, and I thought about how long it was going to take to put everything back in the right places.

"Right, why don't you tell us this Anthony guy's surname, any family or friends he has or if there's someone he might have gone to if he felt threatened," Young Cop requested as he looked at the boxes, carefully avoiding touching them.

"I can't answer those questions," I replied after a couple of seconds to think. "No one ever visited him, and he never told me anything but that his name was Anthony."

There was an awkward pause. Then they asked more questions.

I tried not to worry about how few of them I could answer. They sounded important, and I didn't want to make it harder on them to find Anthony—if he needed finding. The cop had said he might just come back, and a part of me hoped that would happen.

On the inside, I knew it wasn't true, however. Anthony had never missed our Thursday takeout and board game. Not once. Even when sick, he was here.

Over the next half an hour I tried to tell the cops what I did know and how strange this was to get them to actually worry enough.

It wasn't until they found blood under a pile of plates in the kitchen that things got serious. Unable to stay away, I got up to see. There wasn't a lot, but someone had been hurt. Drips trailed along the floor to the sink.

"Looks like someone was here when the place was being ransacked," Young Cop said.

"Not necessarily," the other replied. "It could have been there already. We'll need to get it dated and see how old it is."

"It's fresh. It's on the bottom of the plates," I pointed out before I could stop myself.

I knew it wouldn't help, and the glare I got made it clear they didn't appreciate my input.

"I think it's time we called it in and cordon off the area," Comb-Over said as he walked back through to the rest of the apartment.

Although he looked pointedly at me, I didn't want to leave. I wanted to be there to see if—when—Anthony returned.

They insisted I leave, though, and when I turned to go, something caught the light in some way and it drew my attention. One of Anthony's jackets was slung over the sofa, and I spotted a strange pendant that had half-fallen out of one pocket.

"What's this got to tell us?" Young Cop said as he pushed past me toward it. He'd noticed it when I did. I frowned but didn't to stop him. He grabbed its leather cord and held the pendant up to the light. It was beautiful, but not something I'd seen before. It glimmered in the light as it twisted around. Carved into the stone were three dragons, their bodies and tails entwined and their heads aligned so only one eye was visible on each of their heads.

"Looks like a cult symbol to me. We'd best look it up in the database."

"Cult symbol?" I asked. "Anthony wasn't in a cult."

"I appreciate that you think you know the missing party well, but some things we know well, and people can guard big secrets for a very long time." Young Cop put the pendant in an evidence bag and squared his shoulders.

"Even the people closest to us." Comb-Over motioned for me to continue walking to the door as if he was going to escort me out if required. "We've got your number, and we know which apartment you're in. It's best you leave it to us now. If he turns up, we'll let you know."

"What do you mean, 'turns up?'" I demanded, stopping in my tracks. "Aren't you supposed to look for him?"

"At the moment, it looks like this friend of yours got himself involved in some kind of cult business. While that's a concern—"

The crackle of the cop's radio cut off whatever he was telling me. A woman's voice came out a moment later, explaining something I couldn't hear well enough to make out every word.

She said something about a name search and a check on the apartment as the cop lifted it to his ear, but he walked away from me, glancing back as I followed him.

The other cop reached out to stop me, making me frown again. Before either of us could speak, Comb-Over responded, "Thank you for letting us know. We're going to stick some tape over the door and walk away from this one. Whoever this guy was, as an illegal immigrant, there's no easy way for us to trace him, and if he's involved with a cult as it appears, there's a good chance he's long gone and won't be back."

I gulped, not liking the assured way the cop declared the outcome of this situation. He was making some big assumptions, like that Anthony was an illegal immigrant and was involved in a cult. Anthony couldn't be gone. Why wouldn't they investigate?

Even if I wanted to argue, I wasn't going to get the chance. They both returned to ushering me toward the door and I got the impression it was urgent.

Young Cop pulled out crime scene tape and draped it across the door, and I had nowhere else left to go but my apartment.

I wrapped my arms around myself as the breeze blew through my t-shirt and made me shiver. It was a cold night, and only a sliver of moon hung in the sky above the complex. In one way, I was grateful to be heading to my place.

Despite there being an elevator, I stepped quietly up the stairs, knowing that Mrs. Jenkins might hear if I used it. I did not want her to mother me anymore tonight or keep me from going to my apartment to hide. I felt betrayed and lonely and unsure of what to do.

Anthony had been my rock, and when I entered my apartment, I was met with a thousand reminders of why. He had rewired and replumbed almost everything over the years. At least, it seemed that way.

With no dinner yet and aware that takeout was not really an option given how late it now was, I made my way to my fridge and tried to find something for dinner. I didn't have a lot of choices, but I could throw some stuff into a skillet and fix breakfast of a sort.

As I cooked, I messaged a friend. Stephanie was one of my favorite people on the planet. She'd been in one of the homes I was in for a while, and we'd liked each other immediately. That didn't happen much in my life. She was still in LA, but she had a busy job as a personal assistant, and I didn't see her much.

I told her about finding Anthony gone and his apartment so messed up. Although she knew I was friendly with the handyman, she didn't know how much we shared. It was another reminder that my life was weird when she expressed more sympathy for my being involved than worry about Anthony.

I did get an invite for drinks the following evening, however. Almost instinctively I started to decline it, sure I'd want to be here when Anthony got back. As I sat down to eat, I knew I'd go insane if I didn't distract myself and continued to sit here alone.

I hoped the cops could find him, but what they had said and assumed seemed wrong. With that in mind, I reached for my laptop and searched for the pendant the cops had found in Anthony's jacket. Although I wanted to believe my eyes had been playing tricks on me, I was positive it had glowed.

Whatever it was, it was an important clue, but it wasn't going to be easy to find. There was so much dragon jewelry out there. It was like looking for a needle in a haystack.

It was the only lead I had, however.

CHAPTER THREE

Groaning, I turned off my alarm. My head hurt, and I wasn't sure I'd slept, but I couldn't be late for work again. It happened far too often when the bus was late. It didn't always come on time, and my tardiness upset my boss.

After stretching, I threw back the covers. My arm bumped into the laptop I'd left on the bed beside me. It was still switched on, and it woke up and displayed a picture that was like the pendant I'd seen in Anthony's apartment, but it wasn't the same.

I had found no matches for dragon cults either. In short, it seemed like the necklace might be a dead end.

Worried about Anthony, I continued to feel bad. I had no way of knowing if he was okay or not. And I felt hung over from lack of sleep to boot.

After I was dressed and had made my hair vaguely presentable, I grabbed a bottle of water and an apple. It wasn't much in the way of breakfast, but I worked in a beach shop and café. I would be surrounded by food, especially ice cream, all day. I could eat when I got there.

If I felt like it by then.

I picked up my purse and ran to the bus stop. I often rushed for the bus. I didn't like to get up before I had to.

Although one of the neighbors poked their head out of their door as I thundered past, they didn't call out to me. Usually, my uniform gave them pause.

As I came out of the apartment building, I almost ran into a black car I had not seen in the area before. It was parked in one of the bays that always stood empty. Not everyone living here had a car, but we weren't supposed to use each other's assigned spaces. Some reasoning about knowing it was available for a resident's visitors, if nothing else, which kept people from using each other's slots.

It made me wonder who had a visitor and which apartment the space was for. Mine was in the far corner and in need of attention. Weeds were growing through the cracks in the pavement.

I wasn't going to do anything about it today, however.

Despite cutting it fine to make the bus, my feet took me past Anthony's apartment door and I ran down to open the door again, ignoring the police tape. I wondered why they hadn't locked it. I called his name a couple of times, but there was no reply, and it was still a complete state. Although I was tempted to go inside, I shut the door once more and ran for the bus.

I was just crossing the road to get to the stop when the black car from earlier pulled out of the parking lot and almost ran me over. Although I couldn't see who was inside, I glared at them as I hurried to the other side. A single glance let me know the bus was coming down the road.

Exhaling with relief at not missing it despite my detour, I pulled out my pass and waited for the elderly to be boarded. The beach attracted enough people even on gray days like today that it was never empty, but at least it wasn't the height of summer and the kids were in school, so there was no gaggle of teenagers being macho about strange things.

Male teenagers were the worst. They had too much testosterone and lacked the maturity to realize no one else cared what they thought. Everything was a potential battle, and only swagger and aggression solved problems. It was tiresome.

I thanked the Maker that I wasn't young enough to be bothered by them as much anymore. Most of my friends had grown past that sort of behavior, and the kids on the buses considered me to be yet another boring adult.

The line filed onto the bus quickly. I sat near the back and looked out of a window at the world as it went by. Traffic in LA wasn't great, but it wasn't the worst either. Not that it mattered when I didn't drive.

Normally I loved riding the bus to work. It provided calm and peace and the opportunity to think. Something I loved. But today...today, all I could think about was Anthony. Last night, I'd hoped I'd be able to find him. That the dragon symbol would lead me to him and possibly off on some grand adventure.

I longed for adventure, but I couldn't afford it. Not yet —and besides, college first. It was expensive, but it still led to a better life. At least, I hoped it would. I shouldn't complain. I had the trust fund, and I had a stable life, or I'd had it before Anthony had disappeared.

No matter what I did now to distract myself, I would worry. People had left before now, but this was different. People moved on. Some folks decided they didn't want you in their home when you weren't as clever or tidy as they wanted, or they realized how difficult kids actually were and how much stuff we needed.

But disappearing with the place trashed? from thatAnd blood. I think I'd have been calmer if there hadn't been blood.

I was a third of the way through the journey when the bus lurched and drew my attention back to where we were. We were going around a corner, but it was clear that traffic was bad. As we turned, someone beeped their horn behind us.

When I glanced back, my eyes were drawn to the black car behind us. I frowned, sure it was the one from the apartment block. We were miles away now, though. Could it just be a coincidence?

It was yet another strange event after the night I'd had, and my brain started whirring. What if there was more danger? What if Anthony really had gotten into some kind of trouble? I'd been to his apartment twice now. Had someone seen me?

Shuddering, I tried to push the thought out of my head. I didn't need to think like that. Real people didn't get caught up in conspiracy theories and cults.

It wasn't the kind of adventure I wanted, either. I'd been in the LA area for my entire life. Foster kids didn't get to go on vacations. I wanted to see the country, to go and see the world.

Despite telling myself there was nothing to worry about, I glanced behind us at every corner, trying to catch a look at what was following the bus in every shop window reflection or clean car window.

At first, I was able to reassure myself, but then I saw the car again. And again.

By the time I reached my stop, I'd seen it five times, and it was there when I got off. Fighting my body not to panic, I stayed close to the crowds, grateful that several others on the bus were heading to the beach. I stayed with them hoping it would look like I was part of their group, until we were closer to my work.

I sighed in relief as I ducked under the awning. When I glanced back, the car was gone. It was probably just someone else heading this way.

They probably just carried on, I told myself.

"Scarlet, there you are," Alice said, my boss. "I need you to go get me another box of cones. We're almost out."

I nodded and hid my frown. Given the time of day and how quiet the beach was, they hadn't been replenished the day before. That kind of thing always pissed me off. There was no point in saying anything, however. I needed the job, and this was what I was here for. General gofer. Here to carry, fetch, restock, and serve the customers if we were busy. She needed my muscles far more than my brain.

I got started, fetching the cones and restocking other items that needed restocking. I also served customers when we had a rush and, for a while, I focused on getting through the day.

It wasn't until Alice took a break before the lunchtime rush that I did anything else and then I had the usual grueling half an hour of trying to make the customers happy. It was a welcome break today, however. For thirty minutes, I didn't have to think about anything except giving people what they asked for and taking their payments.

At least, not until an older guy came in, shades propped on top of his head despite the cloud cover we'd had all morning. He ordered an ice cream, so I shifted over to the counter again and pulled on the blue food gloves. I hated them—they made my skin feel clammy—but they were required.

When I went to hand the guy his finished cone, he lifted his arm to take it and his suit jacket shifted. My eyes fixed on a necklace he wore beneath his shirt—three entwined dragons with overlapping heads. Exactly like the pendant from Anthony's jacket.

I gasped, and he took the ice cream from me before I could drop it. He raised an eyebrow as he handed me his payment, then followed my gaze, until he fixed on it as well. He pulled his suit jacket back together.

"Where did you get that?" I asked without thinking.

"Get what?" he replied as I took the money in my hand for the first time. He'd handed me a fifty-dollar bill.

"The dragon thingy on your necklace. It's... strange. I've seen one before recently and loved it, and I wondered where to get one, but I can't find it anywhere." I shut my mouth, knowing I was talking too fast and making myself look like a crazy person.

"It's nothing special," he said, but our eyes locked and I knew he was lying.

Hesitating, I looked at the bill in my hand and then at him.

"A really good friend of mine had one. Only I don't know where he is right now or if he's safe, and I'm trying to make sure he is okay. I'd like to get him a new one."

That made the guy's eyebrow rise even further.

"Your friend is lucky that you care about him so much, but some things are private and have to stay that way. You can't buy a necklace like this, and if he discarded his, that was his choice. Now, can I have my change before this ice cream melts all over my hand?"

"I just want to help my friend," I said. "I'm not trying to muscle in on any secrets. He matters to me. Please tell me what your necklace means."

"No, little girl." He leaned in closer and spoke so quietly that I could barely hear him. "You're asking to know something your friend would rather die than reveal to you."

I opened my mouth to reply, but Alice came through the curtain behind me before I could ask again, and the guy straightened.

"My change, please," he repeated, his displeasure evident in his voice.

A quick glance at Alice made it clear she was paying attention. I could do nothing about this guy and his pendant. With no other option, I made change from the till and handed it to him.

Without another word, he walked out. I sighed as I watched him go.

"What was all that about?" Alice asked.

"I wish I knew," I replied truthfully.

I wasn't sure Alice would let it go. She didn't like us to be even slightly rude to the customers, but more people came in and I went to the stock room to sort through everything and help Alice figure out what needed to be ordered in.

It was a welcome relief to hide in the back while I recovered, but I soon wanted to go back into the store again, curiosity getting the better of my fear. What were the odds of seeing the same pendant twice in two days? Something wasn't adding up.

There wasn't a lot I could do now, though. The guy who'd bought the ice cream was likely to be long gone. And I still had no idea what it meant to Anthony or if I had done the right thing by asking about it. Could I be putting myself in danger?

I suspected the answer was yes, but I wasn't as frightened as I ought to have been. Anthony was a friend who mattered to me. And I wasn't sure anyone else was going to look for him.

A little before closing time, when the beach was less busy again, Alice finally gave the order to get the chairs and the stands of beach toys and postcards back into the shop and start to close.

It would be a while before I got to go home, but this was one of the easier parts of my day, and there was something about knowing I was almost done that made me relax. Despite the weather, it had been a tough day. My mind was elsewhere, and my head and body ached in a way they usually didn't.

I grabbed the first stand with one hand and reached for

the next, having to stretch. When I leaned toward it, I noticed the guy from earlier. He had his sunglasses down now, and he was inclined in the direction of the shop as he leaned against none other than the suspect black car.

As I frowned at him, trying to decide if I should confront him again or be scared of what he might intend, something slipped and fell at my side.

The stand I'd been reaching for toppled over on its own, spilling its contents all over the shop's entrance.

"What was that clatter?" Alice called as she came through to investigate.

"The wind blew at the wrong moment," I said, not sure what else it could have been as I bent to pick everything up.

Alice helped, then went back inside and left me to bring in the stands. I straightened to grab the original one once more and glanced at the road again. The guy and his car were gone. A shudder rippled up my spine as I wondered where he might have gone and what he might have done, but equally, I was glad he had left.

Something was wrong, and despite my desire to find Anthony, I wasn't sure I was ready to know what the dragon symbols meant.

CHAPTER FOUR

After going out drinking with my friends, I felt better. I was also a little frustrated, however. As soon as I'd finished work, I had called the cops to see if they'd made any progress toward finding Anthony. I was told that on investigating both his tenancy and his employment, they'd determined that he wasn't a US citizen but an illegal immigrant and outside their remit to investigate.

I felt sick for him. The cops wouldn't tell me any more since I wasn't family, and I'd had to push for that much, but it was a sure sign they would not look hard for him. He wasn't one of theirs, and no one except me cared whether he was found or not. Their refusal to investigate made no sense.

My friends had encouraged me to let it go. They'd told me he was a grown man and would likely show up as soon as he thought the cops would leave him alone. If he was an illegal immigrant, there was a good chance he was staying away so they didn't deport him.

It was a comforting theory, but it didn't explain the

blood or the guy I'd seen earlier that day. Something still wasn't adding up. Who was that guy? Was he trying to protect Anthony and was keeping an eye on his apartment until it was safe for my friend to return?

But that didn't explain why he had followed me to work and observed me during the day. My only relief was that he'd gone before I'd left. I wouldn't have been able to relax with my friends if he'd followed me there as well.

"Try not to worry," Stephanie said as she hugged me goodbye. "I know he looks in on you, and he seems a really nice guy. But these things have a way of working themselves out."

"Easier said than done, but there's nothing I can do but wait in any case."

"Good. For a sec there, I thought you were going to try to find him. Investigate it yourself or something. That's not a good idea. You don't want to attract trouble. I know we were fearless when we were young, and we've seen more than most, but we need to move toward better things."

I nodded. She was right. I shouldn't look for more trouble, but what if trouble found me anyway?

It was a scary thought, and I pushed it away as I made my way home.

It was a short walk to the nearest bus stop, and at this time of night, it came once an hour. I hurried to the nearest stop, grateful that I knew the schedule by heart. It had rained earlier, leaving behind puddles and wet sidewalks but a city no worse for wear otherwise.

Despite it being a weeknight, there were quite a few people out. This was LA, and the city never slept. Some parts were quieter, like my neighborhood, but the places we went to drink were busier and open late. But I had work again in the morning, however.

I made my way around a couple, their tongues frantically darting in each other's mouths while his hands started to roam up from her waist. Shaking my head at how obvious he was, I smiled and kept going.

When I was several blocks from the stop, the bus went past me, moving fast. I hurried my steps but when it stopped up ahead, only two people got on.

Frelling buttercups, I thought as I ran for it, but I knew I would not make it. I wasn't close enough for the driver to notice me, and the waiting people got on fast. No one wanted to hang around this late.

With no idea what else to do, I slowed again and continued to the bus stop to check. The schedule said the bus had yet to arrive, as I'd remembered. Since when did buses run early?

Even worse, I had an hour's wait until the next one. I considered sitting there. It was chilly but I'd brought a jacket with me. Though if I did, it would be another hour until I got home, and I'd spend the hour wondering if anyone was going to bother me.

I had only the bus fare until I got paid the following day, so I couldn't pop back to the bar and have another drink. No, I was stuck. I could either wait or walk.

Not feeling like sitting with my thoughts in the cold, I decided to walk the bus route. If I got tired or reached an area where I felt safer, I could wait there instead.

With a sort of plan, I carried on. I soon left the area where the stores and bars were open late, and the sidewalk grew quiet. Cars still passed in a hurry, however, and I was grateful the busy street made me focus on crossing at the end of each block.

I couldn't help wondering what Sunday would be like. I often spent time with Anthony on Sundays too. He liked to take the day off, and sometimes he drove me to the beach, further up, where it was quieter.

The idea of sitting around and waiting for him to return didn't appeal to me. I vowed that I'd keep trying to figure out what had happened to him. If nothing else, it would give me something to do. And I didn't think Anthony would mind if I did find him, even if my friends were right about what was happening.

With that in mind, my emotions settled down a little. I was sure I was on the right track trying to find the symbol on the pendant now that I'd seen it on someone else.

Of course, I also hoped Anthony would just come back so I could ask him what was going on. I would tell him what I knew, and my best guess already. If I was close to right, he might tell me. I didn't care if he was an illegal immigrant. He wasn't harming anyone. He worked hard, and he paid his bills and taxes.

Also, he was kind to me. Kind people were rare.

I thought about all the times Anthony had taught me something and all the times I had gone to him with issues I didn't know how to fix as I continued to trudge on, making my way a mile closer to home.

The current area was quiet, the time and distance from the bars and restaurants sending people indoors. My jacket and physical exertion were enough to keep me warm, and I was enjoying having the time to think, so I opted to keep walking. I was halfway home, and I didn't see much point in waiting for the bus now.

It was a dark night, so the puddles here and there barely reflected any light. The moon was the tiniest sliver. I'd always liked the darkness and this period in the lunar cycle. A person could hide in the dark more easily.

Streetlamps stood at intervals, however, but they didn't seem as bright as normal. Almost as if they weren't getting enough power. As I continued on a little further I saw that the next light ahead also wasn't working properly, not casting much of a glow. The next one was dim as well, my shadow almost nonexistent as I stopped between them, frowning. The lights closer to home appeared brighter, so I hurried toward them. I bit my lip as I walked and tensed my muscles. Why was this scary?

When I reached the fourth light since I'd first noticed this peculiarity, it was as dim as the ones before it. Was something strange happening with the lights? I almost laughed at the thought. Lights didn't brighten or dim when someone approached them. At least, not without fancy programming, and why would they do that?

This couldn't be happening. I must have thought the lights were brighter than they actually appeared, or missed one or something. Maybe not even noticed this dim one among the brightness of others. But it kept happening. The lights that had seemed bright when they were further away were dim when I reached them.

I frowned. Was someone playing tricks on me? Why was this happening? Could shadowy government organizations use tech to threaten people?

Fear made me feel cold inside, and shudders rippled

through me. At the same time my legs went numb. I didn't stop walking, however. I went faster instead.

As my heart rate increased, I thanked the stars that I was athletic. Just under a mile to go, and I'd be home. At this pace, in ten minutes, I would be see my apartment block. Another five and I'd be inside and safe.

But the problem grew worse, and the lights got dimmer. I wasn't easily intimidated, so I pulled my phone from my purse and turned on the flashlight.

At first, it shone brightly. Grinning, I thought I had outsmarted whatever was screwing with the lights, but no sooner had I thought this than my phone flashlight also slowly dimmed.

My fingers shaking, I checked the battery, but my cell was almost fully charged. I'd been working so I hadn't used it much that day. Whatever was happening to the light, it wasn't from a lack of power.

I frowned as I tried to figure out what was going on. I could have convinced myself that the streetlamps were malfunctioning, but having my phone act up made the strange phenomenon even more real. My light was a different source. Something external was affecting the light. Something...deliberate.

Seeing no point in having my cell out when it wasn't helping, I turned the light off and put it away. I slowed until my eyes adjusted, then picked up the pace again.

This wasn't how I'd expected my evening to end, but several more minutes later, nothing more had happened. Cars drove past, their lights also dimming as they did, and I realized that had been true for some time. It made me wonder what the drivers thought. Did they realize something was affecting their headlights?

A minute later, I stepped into a puddle, getting water on my pants and washing it up into the tops of my sneakers. I let out a growl of frustration, then saw the water was behaving strangely too. It appeared to be gathering, moving away from the lowest part of the sidewalk toward the middle instead.

For a moment, I couldn't think or breathe. What was happening? How was water moving unnaturally and light disappearing? What was going on? I'd been worried about government organizations or thugs, or cults of violent people who demanded unswerving loyalty to strange beliefs. This looked a lot more like magic. Or insanity. Was I going crazy? Had losing Anthony made my mind break? Was this what people meant when they said trauma had broken them?

I pushed that thought away. In every other respect, I was sane. There had to be another explanation.

The water problem got worse as I went, my eyes just about able to see the water run uphill toward me. I stopped and watched where it was going, wondering if I should follow it to see what was going on.

As I stared into the darkness behind me, I got the feeling that something unfriendly was lurking in the shadows. Fear gripped my heart, and I turned and ran, an almost base sense of self-preservation coming over me. Whatever this was, I didn't want to wait around and find out.

Feeling like I was being stalked by something far worse than the guy I'd been followed by earlier, I sprinted for the next road and the next. My feet splashed in puddles, which were still moving uphill and toward whatever was following me. I could hear the creature as well—a rippling sound gaining on me.

Scared and wanting to hide, I willed the streetlights to get darker and slammed on the brakes to turn the next corner and dart into an alley. There were dumpsters lining one side, and I ducked down between two of them and tried to stifle my breathing. It wasn't easy when my heart was hammering in my chest.

The water moved out of the alley, passing my feet and the dumpsters, and headed toward the street. While I waited it got darker until I could only see the outline of the dumpster on either side of me. Despite the lack of light, I could hear the ripples in the water and then a strange wheezing sound.

Something came closer and closer, inching up the alley I was in, possibly looking for me. If it passed me swiftly, I could think it was just a coincidence and I'd been paranoid. That was what I hoped would happen. If so, everything else could be explained.

But something told me it was after me, and that it wasn't human. Nothing natural made these kinds of noises and moved in this kind of way.

The seconds dragged out like minutes as the source of the noise came closer. Eventually, I saw the outline of a millipede with a beak like a bird's and the head of a feline. It was barely visible in the dark and was swaying from side to side. I couldn't be sure, but it looked as if it wasn't trying to find me with its eyes alone.

The water centered on its body, but also flowed away

again, off down the alley behind it. The creature was unnerving, and I wondered what it would do when it got closer. I couldn't get out of the water and I had nowhere else to back up to, since there was a wall behind me. There was no way I wouldn't be detected by...whatever this was.

I was about to panic when I heard someone splash across the street. The creature whipped around, hissing as it did. Its body moved with surprising speed, the legs making the swishing, rippling noise I'd heard before until it was back in the street and the water's behavior returned to normal.

Waiting for what felt like an age, I gave myself time to recover, letting my heart rate slow and my mind process what I had seen. I felt safe now the creature had scurried off after someone else.

The realization that someone else was in danger smacked into my mind. I winced and slowly straightened. I was safe, and I hoped that whoever the creature followed managed to find a better place to hide than I had.

Either way, I wanted to be home and safe in my apartment, and there was only one way that was going to happen.

I had to brave the night and walk.

CHAPTER FIVE

A sigh of relief escaped my lips as I shut my apartment door, locked it, and leaned against it, not moving. I was safe, and this crazy day could now end. But I knew it was going to be a while before I could sleep. It would be a long time before I forgot the events of the day.

I wanted to go to Anthony. Wanted to tell him everything, knowing he would understand. Instead, I pulled out my cell phone and realized I had gotten a message in the last few minutes. It was from Stephanie.

You home yet, Ladyface?

I grinned at the moniker she used for me. It sounded rude, but it was meant with the utmost respect and admiration, and I adored her for it.

I am. And safe, although it was a close call. I'm not sure what happened. But it was scary.

I typed without thinking and hit send on automatic, but as soon as I'd done so, I wondered if I shouldn't have said anything. How on earth was I going to explain what had happened? It was...like magic. Or like aliens had suddenly become part of my life.

Was that the kind of cult or group Anthony was in? Could they have a link to magic?

No part of me believed in magic, although I knew people who did. Some swore witch doctors and magicians could perform miracles and tarot cards could predict the future. Others had premonitions and stuff.

But I'd never heard of sphinx millipedes that sucked up water and used it to sense prey.

I had to stifle a laugh at the description my head gave me for the creature that had stalked me home and then I jumped as my phone buzzed. Exhaling as my hands shook, and aware I needed to calm down, I read Stephanie's response.

What do you mean, close call? You better be kidding, Scarlet.

I considered telling her I was just joking. I didn't want to put her in danger if something about Anthony had brought this into my world. Although I wasn't sure, I wanted to believe Anthony was the reason all this was happening. It wasn't as if I regularly saw water flow the wrong way.

But then I thought about how scared I was and how little this made sense. I had no idea what was going on except that Anthony had been in danger at some point recently. Maybe he still was. I needed someone to know what was going on other than me. I told Stephanie I'd been followed and how scary it had been. Then I mentioned that they must have had technology that could dim the streetlamps. I left out the description of the creature, making it sound as if a person had followed me instead.

The truth was only important up to a point. I didn't want her to think I was insane, just scared and somehow in trouble. I had no idea what was going on except that Anthony had been in danger at some point recently. Maybe he still was.

She responded immediately.

Oh, hell! That is scary. Do you think it has anything to do with the handyman and you being the one to find his apartment in a mess? Do I need to tell you to be careful?

Stephanie's reaction made me smile, and gratitude swept through me at her comments. I assured her I would be careful and finally moved toward the kitchen to get a snack, make myself a hot drink, and try to settle myself down.

Within seconds, she repeated that I should be *very* careful. I rolled my eyes, wondering if she remembered our earlier talk. I wasn't one to get in trouble these days, and she knew why. State care taught a person to stay off the radar of the wrong people.

But what if they were after Anthony? Or worse, what if that creature, whatever it was, had come after Anthony yesterday? What if it was the reason there was blood on his kitchen floor?

I shuddered at the thought. I had to find out if he was okay. When my phone buzzed again, I was surprised, but Stephanie had more to say.

This might be crazy, but if you think something happened to the handyman and they're interested in you now anyway, you might as well find out what happened to him. Is it worth going back to his apartment and seeing if the police missed anything? If he's alive, he might be able to help you.

The words didn't register at first, and I had to read them again. Was Stephanie encouraging me to get out of trouble by going to look for trouble? It was strange logic, but I liked the idea.

There was a chance that Anthony was safe. Finding him might lead me to safety as well—or get me in further trouble. However, it looked as if I was already in danger.

Thinking about the strange creature made me shudder again. I didn't want to go anywhere with that creature out there, but I still didn't really believe it existed. Could it have been a trick of the eyes? Could it have been nothing but a dog and a strange shadow?

There was no way to know, but I knew my imagination could show me something a lot scarier than reality. Nothing haunted the mind like our own imagination.

With that in mind, I found my backpack and packed a flashlight and some snacks, as well as the rest of my cash. I wanted to be prepared for this adventure to last some of the night. When I was ready to leave, I sent Stephanie another message to let her know I was taking her advice. I wanted someone to know what kind of trouble I was heading into.

> **Good luck. Let me know what you find. If anyone can figure out what happened to him, you can.**

I grinned and straightened my shoulders as I read the reply. Having someone believe in me made me feel a little bolder.

After another quick check of my apartment for anything that would aid my mission, I steeled myself to go forth and face the night and whatever the shadows held.

Making as little noise as possible, I slowly turned the handle on my front door and opened it. I didn't want the neighbors to notice what I was up to. They asked too many questions, and the answers always ended up spreading to the whole block before the day was out.

I walked carefully down the hall, placing one foot in front of the other in such a way as to avoid the worst of the creaks that would give my departure away. It was late enough that a lot of the other residents were in bed, but I didn't want to make more noise than I had to. Once I was in the stairwell, I knew I could move a little faster.

By the time I was out of the front door the sky was cloudless, and it was colder than it had been earlier. I let my eyes adjust to the darkness outside the block and then exhaled. I considered using my flashlight, but I didn't want to draw attention from anyone who might be watching either.

I moved into the shadows by one side of the parking lot and headed to the apartment Anthony had occupied. The police tape over the door looked ragged, as if the weather or cops coming and going had worn it out. I ducked under it anyway and stepped inside.

Staying in the dark for now, I shut the door behind me. The apartment smelled the way it always did and I felt an ache in my chest. I wanted to have Anthony back. I missed him a lot more than I'd have thought I would.

I pulled out my flashlight and switched it on. The room lit up in an eerie way, the shadows making it look different and the destruction and chaos even worse.

I tried not to panic at what might be lurking in the shadows, but my brain tried to project the creature I thought I'd seen in the alley into the shadows of the room.

There's nothing here, I told myself several times and looked again.

I took a couple of deep breaths and waited for my heart rate to slow down. If I was Anthony and I wanted to protect something important or leave me a clue about where to find him, where would I put it?

It didn't take me long to go to the gaming cupboard. That was a cupboard I knew well. The games were the source of most of our quality time together. A lot of them had been pulled out and scattered, but a few had just had the lids pulled off or been knocked out of the cupboard but were still intact.

I had ignored them the first time I'd looked around the apartment since I'd been looking for the handyman himself, not his possessions. Now I sifted through cards, meeples, tokens, and dice, attaching them all to the proper game.

With that checked, I opened the few boxes that hadn't been touched, but I found them all in the same state, if a little shaken in their boxes. Nothing was amiss with these either. Frowning, I straightened, bringing the flashlight beam up with me as I did.

I caught a glint and stopped. Puzzled about what could be drawing my attention to an empty shelf, I slowly lowered the beam of light again, hoping to work out what it had caught on. Had it shone on something innocuous or had I discovered a clue?

Sticking my tongue out and to one side, I reached forward and felt the area where I'd seen the glint. It wasn't any different, the wood smooth. My flashlight didn't give me any indication of what it might have been, but my fingers slowly rubbed a spot near the base of the bottom shelf to the left of the middle.

There was a slight indent, subtle and not visible. It felt different, too. Not quite like wood.

After pausing a moment and trying to decide if I wanted to take this kind of risk, I pressed the indent with my finger. A sharp sting made me try to pull it back, but it wouldn't come away and it only made me ache to try and force it.

I wondered if I'd gotten my finger trapped in a Chinese finger trap. The trick with those was to work it out very slowly and be patient, but I didn't have the time for something like that.

As suddenly as my finger had been grabbed, it was released. I exhaled and pulled it back, relieved and confused. No sooner had I wondered what it had been for than the shelf popped up.

I blinked. This wasn't supposed to happen, but I *had* been looking for whatever Anthony might have left behind, and the games cupboard was somewhere I'd have thought to look. Was I supposed to find this when others wouldn't have? Not sure but determined to find out, I tentatively reached forward. I pried the shelf up. It didn't move at first, but eventually, I got a good enough grip that it shifted. With shaking hands I lifted it.

Underneath was a small compartment, and I grabbed my light to aim it into the gap it revealed. The dust had been disturbed as if several items had been removed. Only one now remained—a small leather-bound journal.

I stared at it. This had been left behind. Had it been left for me to find? I had no way of knowing, but after all this risk I wasn't going to miss the opportunity to work out why.

I scooped it up and opened it. An envelope fell out and fluttered to the floor. Panicking slightly, I redirected the light to see where it had gone. It took me a moment to find it.

The envelope had fallen in such a way that it was underneath the edge of one of the gameboards. I drew it out and saw my name written on it. I *was* supposed to find it. The knowledge made me feel a lot better about snooping around Anthony's apartment.

I tucked the journal in my backpack, sure the letter was more important, and made my way through to the kitchen so I could prop the flashlight on the table and sit on the chair.

Dear Scarlet,

If you're reading this, I want to tell you how grateful I am that you cared enough to look. I'm also sorry, since it likely means that you're alone now and probably a little scared. I know you'll be looking for me. I can't say for sure that I'll be okay or that you will find me, but there's something more important than me now. There's you! I want you to keep looking a little longer.

You may be frightened, and there may be danger, but there's more to you than you would believe possible. Trust yourself, trust your instincts, and don't let anyone stop you from transforming into the amazing being I know you can become.

I'm hoping that a friend of mine will aid you. His name is Ben and he's someone I have a lot of respect for. If he finds you, know that you can trust him.

And always, always follow the dragon.
Anthony.

I sat back, my mind blown. Was this friend the guy who had followed me to work this morning?

Confused but hopeful, I read the letter again. I was about to tuck it into my pack and pull out the journal when I noticed the dripping from the faucet had changed. It got louder and uneven, strange.

My body went cold as I thought back to earlier and how oddly the water had behaved. Glancing over at the sink, I saw that the drops were no longer falling to the bottom of the sink as gravity would dictate. I got up as I heard the door creak. Heart racing, I flicked the flashlight off.

Trying to move silently, I stuffed the letter into my bag.

By the time I moved toward the kitchen door, something was in the shadows in the living room. My imagination showed me the rest of the details. It was one of the creatures from earlier, I was sure.

The room grew even darker, and I inched around the edge of the living room to the bedroom. Not if sure I could be seen or not, I was somehow aware of the creature following me and how it moved. The beast went to the games cupboard, where I had been when I first came in.

I slipped into the bedroom, fear filling me.

I was trapped a monster between me and the only way out.

CHAPTER SIX

I tried to breathe evenly, but my heart pounded so hard I was sure it would be heard. The creature didn't stop at the cupboard but slowly headed around the house.

As it passed across the bedroom doorway, heading across the living room, I held my breath and tucked back a little. I watched it slither almost sideways across the debris and broken furniture.

It appeared to be following the path I'd traveled along. Hoping that meant it would be in the kitchen for a while, I moved to the doorway again.

Fear rippled through me again, freezing me as I saw the tail end of the creature slide into the kitchen. Anthony's warning had been an understatement. This wasn't possibly a little dangerous. This beast was scary and *very* dangerous. This was monsters in the dark, and things that shouldn't be happening. And on top of that, mysterious people carrying dragon pendants kept appearing.

Despite it all, I couldn't panic. Panic would lead to something bad. Or worse—or even death.

I calmed as I heard Anthony's voice in my head, telling me the words in the letter again. If he believed in me, I had a chance.

I stepped into the living room once more. The front door was open, but I didn't want to draw the monster's attention. I had a feeling it was faster than I was, and I didn't want to find out if that was true or not.

I placed one foot in front of the other, my head swiveling from the front door to the kitchen with every step. I heard it slide across the tile floor, then the slight scrape of a chair. No longer moving, I checked what it was up to.

In the light of the moon, I saw the creature sniff the chair I had sat in. My skin broke out in goosebumps as I took another step toward freedom. I had to get out. And before this creature turned around.

There was still a ripped-up couch to navigate around, however. For a few more steps I walked along beside it. As soon as I was past I looked back, but the creature was no longer at the base of the dining chair.

It was by the sink, which puzzled me but not enough to make me stop moving. Whatever had distracted it was giving me an advantage.

I was still a little way from the door when I kicked something. It skittered away from me, making a loud noise. The room turned black.

I somehow felt the creature move behind me without needing to see it. I ran for the door and crashed into more of Anthony's stuff in my scramble to get out. Grabbing the edge of the open doorway with one hand, I steadied myself and kept running. The creature came after me faster than I had imagined possible.

I heard it slithering, a sound from nightmares that helped me run faster. Somehow, I had to reach other people or hide as I had the last time. Sprinting from the building, I headed toward work and the beach on autopilot. I needed to lose this creature.

As I ran, the lights dimmed ahead of me. The cars, streetlights, and buildings all went dark before I reached them.

If I had been running from something normal, it might have been useful to be able to hide in the dark, but it only made it more obvious where I was in a situation like this. Whatever was causing the darkness kept doing so, however. Just my luck that something like this was making it even harder for me. Magic appeared to be normal, and monsters were real, and I couldn't get a blessing of any kind.

My feet thundering along the sidewalk didn't help either, the noise letting it know where to go even if nothing else was. But it felt as if I was finally putting some distance between the creature and me. The monster slowed as I got further from home. I didn't look back, but the sound of its slithering grew fainter. There was a lot less water on the ground than there had been earlier, but it was still flowing past me and toward the creature. Apparently it was water-powered.

I slowed when a stitch formed in my side and lactic acid built up in my thighs, making them seize up. For the first time since leaving the apartment, I glanced behind me. I could see the beaked shadow coming up the route behind me, its path weaving as it followed my trail. Its head and body moved so strangely that I couldn't tell if it was using visual cues to track me or another method.

Wanting to know more about the creature, I crossed the road. I expected the monster to slither across right away, but it continued on a little longer, sniffing until it reached the point where I'd crossed.

I started running again, my footsteps loud enough that its head snapped around. It finally crossed and came toward me, deviating from my scent path. It slowed, however, until it found my scent trail again.

So it's almost blind if not fully, but it can hear and smell me.

No sooner had I realized this than the lights around me brightened, and I blinked. I wondered if the monster had caused this change and I glanced back, but it was hard to see the creature. It shimmered, but its edges were difficult to focus on, like looking at something you could only see out of the corner of your eye. Did that make it a ghost or a creature we'd all seen before but not realized?

Whatever it was, I didn't have time to wonder. We reached a section of road where the surface was wearing out and the puddles were deep. The creature sucked up the water, my shoes splashing in it as it flowed past me.

Confirming my suspicions about the way it used water, the thing sped up.

Despite being exhausted and a growing ache in my legs, I ran faster, looking for higher ground or a building I could get into. But it was the early hours of the morning and everything was locked up. My only option was to find somewhere dry. Somewhere where the creature would run out of water.

I continued running, heading uphill and feeling the ache increase even more. My body started to seize up. The creature had guzzled all the puddles along the way, and the incline made no difference in its speed.

With it gaining on me rapidly, my only other option was to get inside a building, but I was in a residential area. The residents wouldn't let a random stranger inside at this time of night. And that was assuming anyone even opened the door.

I kept running and turned a corner to run on the level. I made my way down two more blocks, glancing back every time I crossed a road. It was now only thirty meters behind me.

I heard it slithering, and it could hear me well enough its path didn't deviate anymore. I had to put a barrier between me and the shadow monster.

I had about given up hope when I spotted a bar whose sign was still lit.

Please be open, I thought, pushing my body hard to get to it before the creature did. It wasn't the sort of place I normally went to, but this wasn't a normal situation.

I had no idea what the monster after me could do, but it might have scared Anthony away or worse. And it definitely wasn't the dragon he had asked me to follow.

I ran through the door of the bar, shoving it open so fast and then stopping so abruptly on the other side that I drew looks from everyone around me.

"Easy there, girl. That door needs to stay on its hinges," someone said from behind the bar. The deep voice only sounded a little irritated.

"Sorry," I replied as I pushed the door shut and backed up, exhaling and letting my breathing slow.

"What can I do for a girl like you this late at night? I hope you haven't gotten in trouble and brought it here."

I glanced at the guy behind the bar. He was in his fifties, with graying hair, and was wearing a denim jacket.

"I've not got into any trouble deliberately, but I'm hoping it won't follow." It wasn't what he wanted to hear, but it was the truth.

I continued to back away from the door, but I still didn't feel safe. I was not ready to trust that the solution to my problem was this simple.

Right on cue, the door blurred and rippled, the wood no longer solid. The creature's head appeared, still difficult to look at in the light.

Several men swore, and bar stools scraped as they leaped up.

"What the hell is that?" the guy behind the bar asked. One patron pulled a gun.

"My trouble," I replied.

I backed up further, putting several tables between me and the monster. Most of the patrons in the bar moved with me. The guy with the gun didn't wait to see if it was dangerous, just fired at it a couple of times.

The bullets went straight through, hitting the wooden door behind it, and the noise startled the creature. Opening its shadowy beak, it let out a combination of a roar, a hiss, and a growl.

If I'd been scared before, I was now terrified. This wasn't meant to be possible. Creatures like this didn't exist.

But here I was in a bar in the early hours of the

morning on a Saturday, with at least five other people, and they saw it too.

Well, sort of saw it.

I looked for another way out, or a way to get around it. It was blind, and it seemed to be overwhelmed by the new smells. The background music was also confusing it.

I didn't want anyone else in here to get hurt because I'd led the monster to them, so I put a finger to my lips. The closest guys gave me a nod and backed up along with me, all of us moving carefully.

Everyone else kept still and quiet. The patron had put his gun away, and the music was the only sound.

The creature paused.

CHAPTER SEVEN

As my body slowly recovered from the run, I watched the liquid in a nearby glass froth and shake. Then water rose out of it, leaving behind a mixture that grew darker and darker in color.

I frowned. This was getting worse. I kept trying to get away from this thing, but it kept following me. Running and hiding weren't working. I still wasn't even sure what it was or what it could do.

Wondering what would happen, I picked up the drink that had been left behind after the creature had sucked the water out of. It was thick and gloopy, and I chucked the remnants at the creature.

When the gunk hit it in the face, it recoiled, then snorted and wriggled.

I couldn't tell if it was in pain or not, but one of the other guys lifted a pint and chucked that.

"No, that will fuel it," I said without thinking. Its head snapped toward me, but it still didn't move, its body now covered in beer.

I retreated until my back reached the bar, watching as the creature absorbed the water and left a sticky residue on its skin. It matched what I'd thrown. Then the shimmering skin rippled, and the gunk slid off the surface, falling through it in places. I exhaled, no idea what to do next.

Nothing was working. I started moving sideways, ushering the men in the bar with me.

"What is it?" the bartender whispered as I got closer. The monster looked our way, the whisper audible over a break in the music.

I shrugged so the guy wouldn't speak again. Everyone was silent until the bartender motioned for us to follow him. He pointed at a door at the back of the building as the monster finished recovering and started sniffing.

After all the extra liquid, it moved swiftly, but I hoped it had to work its way around the tables and chairs like I had and its magic, go through solid objects act was a one off.

The guys ushered me ahead of them, their protective natures coming out. I was being hunted by an unknown type of monster, and we all needed to get out of its way.

The problem with multiple, butch, two-hundred-pound men trying to be quiet, however, was that they had to move slowly. The monster quickly caught up with us.

I encouraged them all to move faster, but we were still behind the bar when someone caught a glass and knocked it off a shelf. The sound of it shattering drew the monster, and it leaped forward. Its beak came down on the arm of the closest guy.

He let out a pained yell as I grabbed the edge of the bar and jumped over it.

"Over here," I shouted.

The shadow beak had really done a number on the limb. The wound was deep and unlike anything I'd ever seen. It didn't look fresh. The edges were seared and oozed a dark liquid. It might or might not have been blood.

The smell hit me a moment later, acrid and pungent. I retched but managed to keep my late dinner down.

That sealed the deal. I didn't want the creature to touch me—not now, not ever.

Feeling guilty, but also in the sights of the creature again, I ran back out of the door. I could feel the creature coming after me, the darkness it carried like a shadow in my mind.

My legs protested after only a block, and to make matters worse, I felt another presence. Something ahead. It felt like the creature chasing me, a sort of atmosphere but one that could be felt with the mind without being seen. I turned right, away from my apartment. I still had no idea how to get to safety.

The respite meant I maintained the distance I had gained, but I was afraid my lead wouldn't last long. I couldn't see stars above, which meant there might be more rain.

If it rained, I was screwed. The water would let it catch me in seconds.

As I rounded the next corner, I saw a bunch of closed restaurants ahead. I wondered if I could hide my scent between their dumpsters as I had before. Maybe it had been a better choice than I'd realized.

I darted down the next alley and spotted the bins. They stank, and I paused for a second, disgusted. The hesitation cost me everything as another of the creatures appeared ahead of me.

Frelling buttercups, I thought and turned toward the bins fast.

I caught myself on the side of the bin, the rucksack I carried hitting the metal containers with a loud clang.

The creatures hissed, two of them now blocking my retreat and one ahead.

Surrounded, with no idea how to defeat them, I felt my body go warm and the alley darkened unnaturally around me. I wanted to hide or, even better, find a way out, but I'd have had to grow wings. So much for finding Anthony and following the dragon. There was no dragon to save me when I needed one.

My body grew even warmer, and I started to pant hard and fast. Was this what a panic attack felt like?

My thoughts raced as the creatures came forward. This was a stupid time to panic. I should have done that the first time I saw one of these things. Or after I'd escaped. When I was safe. That would have been a good time to fall apart.

But I didn't fall apart.

My vision changed.

The shadow creatures became clearer, gained substance, and they got shorter.

No, I was taller, looking down on them and the dumpsters. The smell got worse, and every vile inhalation made my head reel.

I need to get away.

The creatures continued to advance, but they now seemed wary. That, or they knew they didn't have to hurry.

Fly, a voice said in my head. *Fly like your mother taught you.*

I don't remember my mother, I replied, but I unfurled my wings anyway.

The world got brighter, and I felt a jerk in my stomach and the strain of muscles in unfamiliar places. At the same time, the creatures got smaller below me, and the ground was no longer under my feet. They hissed and jumped, but their beaks closed on nothing. My body was too far above them.

I was flying, and I was safe again.

I looked down and back, trying to figure out what was making me float. What new magic was this?

First, my friend went missing, then lights dimmed for no reason, water flowed uphill, and shadow creatures appeared. I found Anthony's letter talking of dragons, danger and chaos. Then more unnatural darkness.

And now this.

When I tilted my head, the underbelly of a deep red dragon came into view, scales shining like well-crafted armor plates. Then I saw the downward sweep of two large webbed wings.

I froze.

Bank, idiot. That voice again. I looked for the source. *And stop shining so brightly. Do you want the whole of LA to see you?*

I snapped my head up to see a building coming up fast.

Frell, I thought again. *Definitely time to bank.*

No sooner had I thought it than it happened, but I still didn't turn soon enough. My underside caught the brick ledge around the roof. It felt rough, but it didn't hurt. The brick crumbled and gave way.

What part of subtle magic do you not understand? the voice demanded again, getting angrier by the second.

The magic part, I yelled in my head.

It growled. Well, my thoughts did. Sort of.

I ignored the voice while I tried to course correct, heading down a busy road. Cars that were still out honked their horns as they slammed on their brakes. Now wasn't the time to argue with a voice in my head.

As I flew, my brain caught up to what was happening. I'd turned into a dragon.

A big red dragon.

And I was flying.

Landing was the next order of business. I was pretty sure I was safe and also sure the drivers on the road didn't appreciate me being above them. Or there at all, really.

Losing control of my breathing, I felt my vision go fuzzy. A park opened up to one side and I banked toward it, trying to figure out how to land.

My mind clouded as I panted too fast to get enough oxygen.

I had enough time to think *frell* once more before my wings clipped some trees, and I hit the ground.

Pain was the first thing I became aware of. Aches and the stings of scratches. Then I felt another presence. This one had no darkness.

When I opened my eyes, the guy from the shop was

there. The one who had followed me to work and then refused to explain the dragon symbol he wore. Refused to believe me when I'd told him I was friends with Anthony.

"You're the last person I want to see," I said as I sat up.

The increased pounding in my skull made me wince. *What had happened to my head?*

"I didn't want to run into you either, but you keep getting involved. Do you know how many rules you broke tonight?"

"I'm guessing more than one?"

"Try five."

"Awesome. Only five." I gingerly got to my feet, looking down as I did.

They weren't scaly or red. They were my normal feet in my normal shoes. I was me. Still. Or again.

"You know, you could have said you were one of us or shown me your symbol yesterday. I wouldn't have shut you out the way I did," he replied as he handed me my backpack.

"You mean the triple-dragons-having-fun-together symbol?"

He glared at me.

"Well, that's one way to put it," he said when I grinned.

"Until Thursday, I'd never seen it before."

He frowned, and it was not the kind of frown that made lines appear on one's forehead. It came with a set jaw and puzzlement. The kind of frown that let me know I'd said something really wrong.

"What?" I asked.

"There's only one type of dragon who doesn't have one of the symbols."

"Sorry, did you say 'dragon'? You did, didn't you? I must have hit my head really hard. Or you did."

He barked a laugh into the night sky, scaring a nearby bird.

"Oh, my skies. I can't believe it. The elders are going to revoke my roaming license. You're an illegal. Someone hid an illegal dragon in LA right under Anthony's nose."

It was my turn to frown. I'd have said I didn't understand, but the trouble was I did understand. I could remember. For a moment I'd been a red dragon and flying away from danger and above cars. Then I'd panicked and hit some trees.

I looked around and winced again. The trees looked like a train had hit them. A dragon-sized train. Some had snapped in half, and I was standing in the middle of a groove in the grass.

"How did I become human again?" I asked.

"You prefer being human," he replied as if that were obvious. "You turned as soon as you passed out. Do you always forget to breathe when you're in dragon form?"

"I don't know yet. Not sure I can call a single event a significant test of the theory."

Again he frowned.

"Come on. We need to get out of here before someone realizes it was us and the council sends in the fixers. With any luck, there will be another red dragon in the area and no one will suspect you."

"You really think so?" I asked, still not sure what he was talking about but wanting him to keep talking now he was explaining things.

"No."

So much for that.

Even if I had no idea what fixers he was talking about, I didn't want the shadow creatures to find me again. Leaving was a great idea, and he might answer my questions about Anthony, if nothing else.

"I'm Scarlet," I said as we hurried out of the park. I hoped offering my name would lead to an introduction.

"Really?" He stopped for a half-second to stare at me, his disdain evident.

"That's what's on my birth certificate," I replied. "What's wrong with it?"

"Bit on the nose for a red dragon, isn't it?"

"Maybe, but I think I got the name first."

He raised his eyebrows but sped up. With his long legs, he looked relaxed, but I was almost running to keep up.

After a few blocks and several turns to keep us out of sight, we reached the black car I'd seen him driving. He went to the driver's seat, and I tried the handle on the passenger door. It was locked. I thought he would leave me behind, but he reached over and popped the lock.

"Thanks," I said, meaning it.

When I sank into the comfortable leather seat, I realized how much my body hurt and how tired I was. It had been a very long day. My companion merely nodded, started the engine, and pulled out.

"I'm going to take you back to your apartment. You need to stay out of trouble. If you don't use your abilities in public again, I won't report this."

"No," I replied, taking a leaf out of his book and not explaining myself.

"It wasn't optional."

"If you have any respect, then respect Anthony's possibly final wishes. I'm going to look for him, and you're going to help me."

He stopped the car and stared at me.

"Do you have any idea how much trouble you will be in if I decide I don't like you? For some reason I don't understand, Anthony does."

"He doesn't just *like* me." I didn't hide my smug smile. "He asked me to find him, and he said I should accept your help."

"Bullshit. You're an uneducated child. And illegal."

I pulled the letter and the journal out of my backpack and my grin grew.

"I found these in a secret hiding place a couple of hours ago."

The guy narrowed his eyes but he took the letter. I enjoyed watching his eyes get wider and his eyebrows rise as he read it.

"So you did know what you are." He handed it back, still not sounding as if he liked me much.

"If you mean I knew about the dragon thing, no, I didn't."

"This implies Anthony knew."

I opened my mouth to make a snarky response but I didn't have one. Being a dragon was a new concept. I didn't have any idea what Anthony had known. I was a mythical beast, and I still couldn't quite believe it was true.

"Am I dreaming?" I asked. "Is Anthony being gone just a horrible nightmare? A realistic but horrible nightmare?"

"How much do you hurt right now?"

"My whole body aches."

"Then what do you think?"

It was a good point. Although I was pretty sure that people in dreams always said they were real, I got the impression that this guy was telling me the truth.

"So, what now?" I asked.

"I have no idea."

CHAPTER EIGHT

"Ben," the guy with me said as he pulled into the drive-thru of an all-night fast-food place.

I was too tired to figure out what he was trying to tell me. The skies had opened, and it was pouring. My brain told me that was important as well.

"My name. If we're going to work together to try to find Anthony, you might as well know my name."

"Oh. Nice to meet you, Ben," I said, my reply genuine since he'd offered to buy me food and talk me through some of what was going on. A moment later, I remembered why his name was familiar. This was the person Anthony had told me I could trust. It went a long way toward helping me relax.

We didn't say any more until he'd bought an insane number of double burgers and he'd parked the car. I was glad we had stayed in the car. Not only did I want to ask him some questions, but the server had been stunned by the quantity of food he'd ordered.

"Tell me everything that's happened the last two days

and what you know, and I'll fill in the gaps," Ben said as soon as he'd taken a bite of his first burger.

Only too happy to talk, I explained the entire chain of events, from finding Anthony gone to being followed by Ben and the shadow creatures.

Although Ben had been annoying in the park, he listened well, not interrupting me and saving his questions for the end. He only interrupted me once to exclaim about three shadow creatures chasing me.

"Is that a lot?" I asked.

"For a young and unimportant dragon, yes. That even one is after you says something."

I frowned. *What could they possibly want with me?*

"Of course, it's possible they haven't found Anthony and they think you'll lead them to him, but that doesn't explain why they're being so aggressive toward you. Nor why so many."

"Then I apparently turned into a red dragon and flew."

"And made yourself shine."

Ben had only to glance at the blank expression on my face to realize that he had to explain what that meant.

"Different colors of dragons can do different things with their magic."

"Like breathing fire?" I asked.

"Contrary to popular belief, dragons don't breathe fire at all. The blue dragons can generate heat or cold and the red dragons can make an area light or dark, not that there are many red dragons left as far as I'm aware."

Understanding dawned on me and I revisited my memories of the last two days and all the lights dimming while the shadow creatures chased me. Because both had happened at the same time, I had assumed they were related, but they weren't, at least not directly.

"Shadow creatures, as you so aptly describe them," Ben continued, "can't change the intensity of lights like you've described. It sounds like your fear and your desire to hide activated your magic. And all this has made it very clear what we need to do next."

Ben gave me a smug smile, and I wondered what he had in mind. Then he took a bite of his fifth burger and looked thoughtful. I waited, but I drummed my fingers on my thighs as I did.

"Okay, new plan. We're going to go to your apartment and pick up some clothes and whatever else you can't live without for a week, and I'm taking you to the elders. They need to know what's happened to Anthony, and we need to get you somewhere safe so you can catch up."

"What about finding Anthony?"

"Can you translate a journal that's written both in the ancient dragon language and in code?" he asked as he started the car.

I shook my head, not even sure where I'd begin.

"Then you need me to handle this bit."

"But you'll let me help if it leads somewhere?"

"I can't promise to. If I take you in, then you need to understand that the elders will have the final say on what happens to you and what you can and can't do. There are rules in our society, and you apparently have a lot to learn. But it will keep you safe until we can find Anthony."

"All right. I'll come willingly, although I don't like the sound of all of it." I didn't want to have to follow any arbitrary rules or agree that a group of elders I hadn't met could decide my future. Telling Ben I wasn't fully on board prepared him for me disagreeing with their decisions later.

Ben headed to my place without directions. Then he insisted that I stay in the car while he did a sweep of the area for more shadow creatures.

"There is one in Anthony's apartment," I said, feeling the same strange dark presence I did when they were close.

Once again I was both grateful and not for the rain we'd just had. It had probably washed away my scent and made it hard for the creatures to locate my apartment, but it also meant they had plenty of energy to draw on. Despite my words, Ben got out of the car and went to check.

When he came back, he confirmed that indeed, there was a creature in Anthony's apartment.

"Did it sense you?" My eyes went wide as I thought about being chased by another, but Ben shook his head and stopped my fear in its tracks.

"How did you know, and from so far away?" Ben asked.

"I can feel them. Can't you?"

"Not very well. I'm starting to understand Anthony's interest in you."

I didn't know what to make of this statement. Anthony had been a friend. Was there more to his friendship with me than it had seemed?

"Will you do something for me?" he asked. He motioned for me to be quiet as we snuck into the main block of apartments. I thought it was a little unfair that he asked me a question and then cut me off from responding. I wondered what he would say when we were inside my apartment.

"Don't mention being able to sense the evil after you as

well as you do if you value your safety," he told me after the door was shut.

"That's cryptic," I replied as we took the stairs up, moving silently more than swiftly.

"It's all I can say until we find Anthony or whatever he's been looking into."

Although I wanted to demand answers and to understand everything, I saw the merit in Ben's words. Whatever Anthony had been up to, it would be good to be careful until we had a better idea. Or he was back.

As I packed a small suitcase, I messaged Stephanie to let her know I had found something and might be away for a few days. Then I sent a message to my boss, claiming to be very sick.

"How long does it take to throw some clothes into a bag?" Ben called from the living room, making it clear that I was out of time.

I sighed and shoved my cell phone into my pocket, then chucked my deodorant into my suitcase, along with my hairbrush. Making a quick mental note of everything I'd already packed, I wondered if I'd forgotten anything.

There was a knock on my bedroom door as I zipped the bag closed. Ben opened my door and came in without waiting for a response.

"We need to hurry up." He glanced at my bag and nodded, satisfied. He picked it up, and I rushed after him, insisting that I could handle my own luggage. That amused him more than anything else so far.

"You really *don't* know much about dragon culture, do you?" he said.

"I didn't even know I was a dragon until a few hours

ago. Anthony never mentioned..." My voice trailed off as I processed what that meant. "Is Anthony a dragon?"

Ben chuckled as he nodded. I wasn't sure if I should be blown away by having it confirmed or still be in shock that dragons were real.

"Anthony is one of the best dragons, and I hope he's still alive to tell you more one day."

'You and me both," I replied. "But I still have no idea what that has to do with me not carrying my own bag."

Ben merely blinked, not appearing to follow the conversation. I opened my mouth to explain, but he caught up to what I was saying.

"Oh, In dragon culture, we know women aren't weak. I took your bag for speed and to give you the space to think about what you might have forgotten."

I closed my mouth with a snap, not sure how to respond to something so accepting and helpful. I hadn't liked this guy when I'd first met him, but he could have been a lot worse.

After confirming that I had everything, we returned to his car. Along the way Ben asked me what I sensed, but the presence was still in Anthony's flat, and we reached the car and got out of the parking lot before it realized we had been there.

"Where are we going?" I asked when Ben made his way onto the nearby freeway.

"A dragon city. It's further up the coast. Hard to get to and even harder to find if you're not one of us."

I exhaled, not sure I completely believed it. It seemed like a crazy response. I was pretty sure humans had been everywhere. How could a city be hidden from view? Surely satellites had spotted it, even if others had not come upon it.

When I voiced those concerns, Ben laughed.

"You'll see." He flicked on the radio. "Sleep if you need to. We're going to be driving for a while."

I considered asking my questions again, or more specific ones, wanting to get him talking, but he drove on and I couldn't bring myself to. Instead, he asked me how I'd met Anthony. I didn't want to admit I had a trust fund, finding it caused a lot of awkward conversations, so I focused on being alone and needing help to learn how to manage as an adult.

"Sounds like he connected to you right away," Ben said.

"Something like that."

"We'll find him. He's strong and powerful. If he got away from the apartment, he probably made it to somewhere safe."

"Then what would he do?"

Ben frowned and didn't answer right away, and not because he had to concentrate on traffic. We were on an almost empty freeway. He wasn't sure how to answer.

This made me worry all the more. Anyone who appeared to know Anthony as well as this Ben guy did ought to have some idea.

"I'd hoped he'd contact me by now. It bothers me that he hasn't. But either way, he's a powerful dragon, and he'll be safe somewhere. I'm sure of that."

At no point while Ben spoke would he meet my gaze. His eyes were fixed on the road, and his knuckles were white as he gripped the steering wheel. I couldn't think of any more questions as we drove into the early morning and the first stage of dawn.

The sun was almost entirely to our right when it crested the horizon. Ben had been driving through the middle of nowhere for so long that I was sick of seeing the same sights, and sleep hadn't come, worry too fresh in my head.

"What were those things chasing me?" I finally asked. I felt safer talking about the monsters that went bump in the night when it was light out.

"Shadow catchers."

"'Shadow catchers?'"

"Yeah. Water-powered. They feed on the soul, and if they'd caught you, they'd have sucked enough of it out of you that you'd want to die if they didn't take it all. They're almost entirely mindless and sightless, especially during the day. Don't let that make you complacent, however. They can smell and hear much better than humans."

It was my turn to frown.

"They struck one of the men at the bar, and it looked as if his flesh had melted," I said, shuddering just thinking about it.

"Yeah. Wounds decay like weeks have passed in the blink of an eye. If he survived and it wasn't too deep, he might recover without a problem. It depends what he does to feed his soul and how healthy it was in the first place."

"How healthy his soul was?" I asked. I had no idea what that meant or how anyone could be sure they had a soul.

"Yeah. Like the body, if you do things that nurture your soul, the healthier and hardier it becomes. Creativity, being kind to people, showing compassion, making decisions that lead to the betterment of the planet—those all go into the makeup of your soul. A good strong soul can stand up to a shadow catcher and its masters far better."

"Its masters?" With every word that Ben said I grew more worried. What had I gotten myself into?

"Shadow catchers serve another entity. It's not something you have to worry about right now, I swear. There isn't one at large."

"Even with three shadow catchers?"

"Even with three of them. I think Anthony attracted them. They were probably looking for him and thought they could follow you to get to him."

I exhaled, aware that Ben had said something similar before. If he was only trying to reassure me, I didn't want to know.

"Anyway, we've almost reached the city. You can get all your questions answered by people who know much more than I do." Ben had relaxed his grip on the steering wheel, but he was sitting further forward as if he were looking for something.

I considered asking him what he was looking for, but then I remembered he had mentioned a dragon city. I didn't want to display any more ignorance about the dragon world right now. There was something about the way he'd talked of it that made it sound like this was an important place for the dragons in this world.

I set my jaw as he sped up. It looked like he was going to drive straight off the road where it turned a corner to avoid a cliff. He hit the throttle, and I dug one hand into the leather upholstery on one side of the seat while grabbing the oh shit handle with the other.

"Ben?" I asked when he'd pushed the car as fast as it would go.

"Don't panic," he replied, grinning as he glanced at me. "You're a dragon, remember? You can fly. Even if we hit the ground or landed in the sea, you'd be fine, just like earlier."

As much as I wanted to believe him—I remembered hitting a building and not feeling it, as well as crash-landing on some trees in a park in the middle of LA and walking away—this wasn't comfortable. Screwing up my face, I closed my eyes and held on tight. The cliff edge was only a few meters away now.

"Do you think you could not make us glow like the sun in the middle of the desert?" Ben asked as he slowed again. "And you might want to open your eyes."

Not sure I agreed, I kept them closed and focused on what I felt. The car was still running but Ben was continuing to slow. If we had gone off the cliff road then we'd have hit the ground already.

I relaxed my face, and when I was calmer, I opened my eyes. My heart started hammering in my chest again as I gawked at the dragon city before me.

Built half out of the natural cliff as it extended out to sea, the dragon city partly floated on the water, what appeared to be several miles of coastline visible either side of it. The dragon city partly floated on the water and was partly built into the edge of the cliff face.

"Welcome to Detaris," Ben said. "Home of the dragons and their kin, and the place where you're going to learn all about us."

"It's beautiful," I replied, looking around.

It was mostly built of dark-gray rock. The land dropped

away on both sides of the road leading to it, making it defensible. The buildings merged into the cliff, and everything was in harmony with the nature around it. There were towers and turrets on large houses as well as smaller ones designed for those in human form, clearly not big enough for the dragons. Everything looked as if it somehow belonged.

The center was so tall and looked so strong that it appeared to be a castle among the clouds. If I hadn't believed in magic or dragons before now, here was more than enough evidence to change my mind entirely.

As the car closed on the city, still slowing, I gaped. The dark stone would have looked oppressive and dreary if not for the lights blazing everywhere and the way the sun lit up the stone, glinting and sparkling on something woven into it. Instead, it looked like a fairytale of brightness and movement.

Dragons in both forms were everywhere, their bright scales of various hues adding to the scene. We'd been noticed; several people in dragon form moved onto the road that ran up toward the center of the large tower in the middle.

CHAPTER NINE

Ben pulled to a stop in front of the largest black dragon I could see. I waited to work out if I was supposed to get out of the car. Within a second Ben pulled out my suitcase and his bags, then gestured for me to get out.

As I opened the door, the black dragon crouched and brought his face close to Ben's.

"You've brought another young one in with you." The deep rumble of the dragon's voice was almost intoxicating.

"Yeah. Anthony was looking out for her. She hasn't got any family, and she's unregistered. Will you help me get the paperwork?" Ben picked up his bag as if nothing was wrong with this request and it also wasn't important.

"Depends on whether you found Anthony or not."

Ben looked up at the dragon. I continued to look between them, standing a little way back and clutching the small case as if it held everything that mattered to me. Admittedly, it came close, but showing emotions and information like that to people had always seemed like weakness when growing up. I did my best to relax.

"He's still missing." The dragon dipped their head, answering their own question.

"There were three shadow catchers for sure and no sign of him," Ben confirmed.

"Nothing to suggest where he's gone or why so many were hunting him?"

"No," Ben replied. I opened my mouth to say the opposite and mention the journal, but Ben went on. "There was nothing. He's vanished. I might have one small lead, but it's a long shot, and I need the library here. You know how he liked to play with languages."

"I do. He made sure we preserved a record of our language, among many other things, and for that he has my respect."

"He likes to be useful. I like being able to focus on a single task. I want to check out a theory, and I need to drop off this dragon so I don't have her asking me questions every five seconds."

I put a hand on my hip and began to ask them what they thought they were doing by talking about me as if I weren't there, but I didn't get a chance to say anything about that either.

Another large dragon touched down, making it look effortless, barely producing a sound. The sun gleamed off their ivory scales, making me squint against the brightness.

"Is this the dragon that wrecked downtown LA, used magic in front of several humans, and then had the stupidity to take dragon form where anyone and everyone could have seen her?" the ivory dragon asked.

"Capricia, you know it could have been way worse. It's difficult for a young dragon without good control of their powers to escape from three shadow catchers. It could have been way worse. It is a miracle that she's still alive and everyone else is too." Ben stepped forward and inclined his head toward the dragon. She touched her forehead to his.

"That may well be, but we've had to get the fixers on it in overdrive. And no one likes dealing with a cranky fixer."

Ben shuddered and stepped back. Finally, the dragons looked my way, acknowledging me for the first time.

"You should go to check in and get registered," Capricia said. "And then you need to report to the chambers for more information. I knew Anthony was working on something he felt was important. But whatever he was working on, it was more dangerous than he informed us of, it seems."

I gulped.

"Come on." Ben hooked his hand through my elbow to guide me.

Grateful to have a tour guide in this new place, I let him steer me away. I also had questions. He hadn't shared the existence of the journal I carried in my bag. What was I supposed to do with it if no one but him knew about it?

As soon as we were away from everyone, I intended to ask, but more dragons landed. Some nodded at me, and I tried not to worry about how intimidating they were, reminding myself that I was one of them. That was easier said than done as one particular pale-yellow dragon landed only a few feet away. I gasped and jumped back.

They turned into a young man wearing a ripped t-shirt and torn jeans. He had platinum-blond hair, which he ran his hand through as he stared at me.

"Didn't mean to startle you." His voice was surprisingly gentle. "You're new?"

"You could say that," I replied warily. I never said much to people I didn't know well.

"Flick," he introduced himself. He stuck his hand out for a shake, then pulled it back and wiped it on his t-shirt before holding it back out.

I took it and gave him my name, but I didn't offer him any more than that.

"See you around, I guess," he added, then turned and walked off the edge of the road. I inhaled in surprise and went over to look down.

As he fell, he transformed again until he was a yellow dragon once more and soared through the sky. I watched him with my mouth open as he ascended and wheeled around the city. Then I shut it with a snap and turned back. Ben had folded his arms and was grinning.

"What?"

"He was showing off. Got yourself an admirer already."

That made me frown more than anything else could have. Guys complicated things. Their egos got in the way, and they tried too hard to get laid and not enough to connect. At least, that was what my experience had always been.

"You'd best take me to get registered," I replied, wishing I hadn't watched Flick fly for so long. I didn't want to encourage him.

Thankfully, Ben said no more about it. He led me through narrow walkways only a human could traverse. I noticed that deeper into the city, there were lots of carved or neatly concealed rope bridges that allowed human-form dragons to move between the taller buildings without having to come back down.

I once again stared open-mouthed at the beauty around me.

"Because we have to conceal this settlement, we've kept it compact, with only a few areas where we can stay in dragon form. It means the city is smaller, and we can have visitors from other races if need be."

"Other races?" I asked as we hurried up some stairs and then out of a door and over a carved bridge with wooden paneling.

"You don't think only dragons and humans inhabit this planet, do you?" he replied.

I opened my mouth to remind him that I hadn't believed in anything but humans two days earlier, but then I caught sight of his face. He was grinning from ear to ear, teasing me.

"You'll learn about all sorts and have your questions answered at the academy, so I won't waste my breath telling you about them all."

"Academy?"

"Yeah. You may be an adult in human eyes, but in dragon terms, you're a child, and you've missed a lot. Even if you were an adult dragon you'd be enrolled, and someone would claim guardianship of you until you were done and able to show you were equipped to be considered a dragon adult. I hope that's not going to be a problem."

I shook my head without hesitation. The idea of learning at some kind of school didn't make me feel happy about coming here, but I was curious. I wanted to ask someone what was going on and what this whole place was all about. Who knew when I could start at the academy, though?

Ben hurried me along more bridges and up more stairs until I was out of breath and my arms ached from carrying my luggage. It was weird seeing dragons outside, but the interior halls were almost empty.

"How much further?" I paused at the bottom of yet another spiral staircase. I was ready to swear off anything with any sugar in ever again if it would make me fitter.

Already on the third step, Ben turned back as if he had just noticed I was following him.

"Are you struggling?" he replied, his curiosity and surprise genuine.

"No, I just wanted to bitch. We're halfway up the tallest tower ever known to man, and I want time to count the cracks in the walls."

Ben lifted an eyebrow and came back down, holding out his hand to take the suitcase.

"You need to embrace your inner dragon. It makes things like this easier."

"They must have missed that topic when I went to school." I grinned and let him have my bag.

To my surprise, he hefted it as if it were nothing and kept on walking. I had no choice but to follow, tired and still aching.

While I followed after him, I thought about what he'd said. Could I really tap into some internal power and make this easier? While carrying my case, Ben wasn't out of breath and didn't break a sweat. He strode up and over several more bridges.

We were now a long way up, and I could feel the strong

breeze and cold every time we moved from one tower to the next. I started to suspect that Ben was making a fool out of me when we came back to the central tower for the third time.

I pointed at it the fourth time he brought me back to it.

"What kind of tour are you taking me on? The see-everything-and-walk-the-entire-universe tour?"

"No. The avoid-everyone-who-doesn't-take-kindly-to-unregistered-illegals-and-would-take-advantage-of-you-not-being-protected tour. We're almost there."

Although Ben spoke calmly, he glanced to our right as we entered the next tower and looked down the stairs. I heard arguing somewhere below us, and Ben put a finger to his lips.

I wasn't going to take any chances, so I followed him as silently as I could up the stairs and across one final bridge to a set of double doors. Ben put my suitcase down and paused with his hand on a doorknob.

"Don't say a word about the journal you found. They hopefully won't ask you about it, but it needs to stay hidden. Do you understand?"

Ben said the words so quietly I could barely hear them, but I nodded. He'd meant every word, and I didn't need much encouragement to keep from trusting most of the people I met. I only trusted Ben because Anthony had told me I should, and to follow the dragon. In my experience, most people couldn't be trusted. It was good to know that someone felt the dragon world was no different. When we heard people coming up the stairs behind us, still arguing, Ben pushed the door open and gestured for me to go inside. His eyes flicked to the stairs again, and his mouth set into a firm line as the people came into view.

The first was a tall, thin guy wearing a leather jacket. He was older, and his hair was slicked back. The way he carried himself said he had strength and knew how to use it.

When the new dragon stopped at the top of the stairs the atmosphere shifted. Ben tensed and stared at the newcomer. With him was another man. His garb and accessories marked him as different. He wore a tweed jacket and dress slacks, and he had a book tucked under his arm like a college professor.

Like mine, his eyes flicked between Ben and the first guy.

"Well, I need to get back to my work. I'll talk to you later, Neritas."

Neritas nodded acknowledgment, then his eyes locked on me.

"New blood?" he asked, taking a step closer. He stayed focused on me, despite directing the question at my companion.

"New here, but not to the world of dragons. Anthony has been with me in LA for several years." I lifted my chin. *Don't show weakness or fear*, my mind screamed, reminding me what it could cost me to do so.

"Not registered?"

"She will be in about two seconds. Go on, Scarlet. Neritas shouldn't keep you." Again, Ben motioned for me to go inside.

"You'd best come too, Ben," I replied, grabbing his arm

as if I were in a relationship with him. "They'll want to hear your side of things."

It was the biggest bluff I'd ever made, and I had no idea if it made sense. Ben exhaled with relief as we hurried into the room and the door swung shut behind us.

The room was grand for a place that sat at the top of a very tall tower, although it contained only a single desk. It was three-quarters of a circle, give or take, and the floor was tiled in the same dragon pattern the amulets bore.

A woman was sitting behind the desk. The device before her looked like a modern computer with a detachable screen, but something wasn't quite right about it. It was working on its own while she stared at it.

Ben walked over to her, his shiny shoes clacking on the floor. I moved more delicately, not wanting to draw attention to myself. She finally looked up, glanced at Ben, then fixed her eyes on me.

"New one to register?" The question was not directed at me, although she looked me up and down a couple of times.

"That's about the size of it."

"You're a bit old to be a new registrant, aren't you? Your family lives in another country?"

I shook my head.

"No. Anthony found her. I thought it was time she came in and got a proper education."

The woman frowned and straightened an almost perfectly straight spine. Her suit rippled and seemed to change color when she moved. She rearranged the tablet in front of her and stared at the screen again.

"Right. Parents?"

"Dead," I replied. I was used to telling people I didn't have parents. "As far as I know, anyway."

"Their names, then? What color were they?"

"Don't know their names or their color. Didn't even know they were dragons until a day ago."

The woman sat back and looked at Ben as if I were joking.

"She's an illegal," Ben said.

"And how am I supposed to register someone who has no parents in the database? I would have no idea where to begin looking."

"Register her to me if you need someone." Ben shuffled his feet from side to side.

If nothing had shocked the woman so far, this did. The screen on the table flickered, and her mouth dropped open for half a second.

"I take it she's blue then?"

"No." Ben winced.

"You know as well as anyone that for a dragon to be registered to a parent, they have to be the same color."

"I'm red," I replied, wondering what the fuss was about. The woman's mouth dropped open.

"Pure red?" she asked, her voice quiet.

"I think so. I didn't see me, but I assume so. What's wrong with that?"

"There aren't many red dragons in the database," Ben said.

"Not alive, anyway."

"Then my parents probably *are* dead." I shrugged. This had gotten awkward. I got the feeling that something wasn't being explained to me, but no one even tried to and now Ben wouldn't look at me. His left hand clenched up into a fist, and he jammed his right hand deep into his pants pocket. He studied the ground for so long I wondered if he was ever going to talk to me again.

"Do you have a date of birth?"

I shook my head. "I don't know that for sure either. They think I was born in June in ninety-five, but they don't know more than that."

"Well, pick a day. Something has to go into the database. I'll have to list you as an illegal and can only partially register you. That will allow any possible parents to come forward to claim you, but it will also let everyone know you're unclaimed."

"You can't register her to me in some way?" Ben asked.

The woman sighed and looked at him again. "I understand your concern, but we both know that if she's to thrive in the long term, finding her parents is the best way forward."

Ben bent down and spoke in a quiet voice. "And we all know that for any other color, that wouldn't be a problem. But there aren't many red dragons alive."

"What's wrong with my color?" I asked, folding my arms across my chest. "Why is red so bad? Did one of my ancestors murder everyone or something?"

"No. Your ancestors were royalty. Some of them, anyway. The rest were a mix of exiles, illegals, and dragons who have never wished to live in our society."

"Oh," I replied. "I'm pretty sure I'm not royal. I think that's something royalty knows about."

"All of us would."

"Then my parents were probably illegals or didn't want

to live nearby." Once again I felt as if this was all going horribly wrong, but my words smoothed everything over, and within ten minutes, we were done and Ben ushered me from the room.

"That didn't go according to plan," Ben said a moment later.

"I'm not sure what the plan was," I replied, not hiding my annoyance. At the same time I put my bag between us.

"Sorry. I was hoping to get you registered to me. There's something about you that Anthony wanted to hide, and I don't know what. Your color is a thing, but it's not the only factor involved."

"Well, I'm not hiding anymore."

"No. You're not. Everyone will know about you by the time I get you to a guest lodge."

Ben's words should have been nothing new. The homes I'd been in as a child had been the same, but there was so much sadness in his eyes that I knew something deeper was at play. I knew I was not going to like it.

CHAPTER TEN

As I looked around the small room I'd been assigned, I sighed. It was smaller than my apartment in LA, but it had a cozy feel to it.

Ben still stood in the doorway as I surveyed it.

"Sorry we couldn't get you something on a higher floor and nearer the academy classrooms."

"I got the feeling she didn't want me any closer," I replied, thinking back to the reaction of the person in charge of assigning the guest rooms. I was an illegal and of unknown parentage, dragon scum.

"I can't pretend this is going to be easy on you," he warned me. "But you've got to understand that this is where you belong in a lot of ways. And no matter how hard it is, it's really important that the human world doesn't find out about us. Dragons are dead as far as the world is concerned, if they ever existed. It has to stay that way."

"Why?" I tucked my suitcase in the corner and decided to unpack later.

"The academy should explain that."

"Is that your way of saying it's complicated?" I asked as I grabbed my purse and checked that it had basics like tissues and a bottle of water in it. The journal and letter Anthony had given me were also inside. Wherever I went, it was coming with me.

"There's a lot of good reasons that I don't have time to explain when I am supposed to be trying to find Anthony. Also, can I photograph that journal so I can try to figure it out?"

I pulled it out and let him snap photos of some of the pages with his phone. I was grateful he didn't want the physical book. Anthony had trusted it to me, even though he'd trusted Ben, and Ben appeared to care about Anthony.

"Right, I'm going to the library. If you need me, I'll be in the south wing. I will make sure the librarian knows you're aiding me with research so you can find me without trouble. I can't promise that will get you admitted, but it should at least get them to tell me you stopped by."

Ben's statement gave me more questions than answers, but he didn't say any more. He hurried away, leaving me in the small room with a bed, a closet, a desk, and a large chest sitting open at the end of the bed.

Not sure what else to do, I decided to go to the academy and try to figure out where to enroll. I wanted to find Anthony, but first, I had to learn a lot more about who I was and what was going on.

Although I wanted to insist that Ben teach me everything, I got the feeling he wanted to be alone. I'd never liked being idle, and learning appeared to be my only good option.

I left my room, shutting the door as I left, but there was no lock. I frowned, but I couldn't do anything about it now. This place wasn't conventional.

With nothing else to do, I looked for the academy tower. It wasn't easy to spot, lost in the maze of buildings, but I eventually figured out how to get to it.

I opted to stay out in the open at the bottom of the city and climb the tower when I got there. I crossed several bridges that stretched only a few meters above the crashing waves. The heavenly sound echoed through the towers, but it wasn't overwhelming.

I looked at the buildings as I walked, staring at all the different designs. None were the same.

After walking for a few minutes, Flick appeared, jumping down onto the bridge in front of me and blocking my way. He didn't hide his roving gaze.

"Scarlet, right?"

I nodded and kept my eyes on him, wondering what he truly wanted. There was something about men with a lot of bravado. It often hid a deeper insecurity.

"You look lost."

"Just heading to the academy to register. Apparently, I've got classes to take," I replied casually.

"You really are a non-registered then?" he asked, his eyebrows lifting for a fraction of a second.

I bit the inside of my lip. He'd just confirmed that everyone was already talking about me. I wasn't unregistered anymore, though, and I pointed out as much.

"You *were* a non-registered. Huh. It's a culture shock to come here when you've been outside for so long. Why don't I fly you up to the academy and show you around?"

"I'm good, thanks. I'll take the stairs." I tried not to show my fear. He was still blocking the way to the stairs, and he knew it. He glanced at the tower behind me and the few steps that could be seen through the open doorway.

"Really want to climb that whole thing?" he asked.

"Yeah. I do."

"Because you can't fly yet?"

The question stunned me. Even if it hadn't been so close to the truth, there was something about it that seemed rude.

"Look, I had a shitty night. I was chased by not one but three shadow catchers. I hardly ate, and no one has yet told me where I might find food here. I haven't slept since getting up for work yesterday morning. All I want to do is the crap I have to do to register, and then I want people to leave me alone so I can catch up on sleeping and eating.

"I get that you and a bunch of other dragons in this place are super curious about me. Or you might not be, and I'm the perfect person for you to pick on to make yourselves feel better. In either case, I'm not in the mood for any of it. So, get out of my way or find me a burger...or something."

I crossed my arms over my chest and squared my shoulders. I wasn't sure where I had found the guts, but I knew if bullies were overhearing this, it was the best way to show I wouldn't be an easy target.

With every sentence I spoke, Flick's eyes got wider and wider. Finally, he stepped back and motioned for me to go ahead.

"Thank you," I added as I took advantage of the gap and headed for the many stairs I had to climb.

I had barely enough room to get past him, but I carried on anyway, trying not to brush up against his chest, pretty sure that was what he wanted.

Thankfully I was thin and I could squeeze through the gap without contact. I hurried up the first flight of steps, trying to put distance between us.

After three flights, I had to slow down. My legs still ached, and my heart rate was higher than I wanted it to be. If I pushed my body too hard, I wouldn't have anything left to run away with later, if I needed it. Not that I thought I would, but what Ben had said about my current status had left me worried.

I slowly climbed the next few flights, spiraling around and around as the tower widened and got busier. A few dragons in human form looked my way, and one or two of them stared, but no one stopped me or tried to hinder me.

It was a relief to move around freely after what Ben had told me. Still, I tried not to draw attention to myself as I headed up.

I was still a long way from the academy when another familiar dragon appeared in front of me. Neritas had come down the stairs quietly enough that I didn't hear him until he stood almost right in front of me.

"Well, well, well. If it isn't the little runt Ben was protecting earlier," Neritas said, his eyes fixed on my face.

"Whatever you're planning, get it over with, so I can go register at the academy," I replied. Someone came up the stairs behind me and stopped so that I couldn't retreat.

"You think I'm going to do something to you?" He took a step closer as he spoke, entering my personal space.

"Ben seemed to think that you would, given half a

chance. And as you can see, I'm between you and..." My voice trailed off as I glanced behind me.

The dragon behind me was staring at my butt, but when I looked over my shoulder, he glanced up and blushed. His thin frame was lost in a robe like that of a monk or an apprentice. I rolled my eyes at his obvious leering.

"Stevie, get lost," Neritas added as I looked back at the stronger looking of the two men.

The dragon behind me didn't say a word but went back down the stairs. I fought not to show fear. Neritas had me right where he wanted me and he knew it.

"You've got a lot of guts and a good mind too. You didn't run, and you're not stupid enough to attack me either."

"Thank you. I think," I replied as he relaxed.

"There was a time when I'd have enjoyed making someone like you feel scared. And there are plenty scaring you. Most believe I'm still like that but..."

"Something changed all that?"

He gave a single flick of his head up and down and looked me in the face. "You're a red dragon, right?"

"Apparently. What's that got to do with why you're not being mean?"

"It's a complicated story and not one I want to talk about here. One day, maybe I'll tell you. In the meantime, when trouble comes, if it's more than you can handle, come find me. I'm on the north side of the city at the top of the corkscrew tower."

I lifted an eyebrow.

"*When* trouble comes, and *if* it's more than I can

handle?" I asked, emphasizing those words to make it clear that I was intrigued by his choice of words.

"Being a red dragon is both a blessing and a curse in this time and age. It's clear you know something about keeping yourself out of trouble, but trouble will come."

"Between you and Ben, I'm starting to think I shouldn't be here. Sounds like I should go back to the normal world and take my chances."

"With three shadow catchers after you?"

The gossip mill worked well in the dragon city, but he had more of a point than I liked. The shadow catchers would still be a problem when I went back.

"Let me walk you up to the academy to register. I can answer some questions and keep you safe that far." Neritas moved out of my way.

It wasn't what I'd expected when I saw him. However, it would give me some protection, and if Ben was semi-scared of this dragon, it might be better to cooperate for now. I wouldn't let my guard down, however.

I fell in beside him, grateful that he took the inside section where the stairs were narrower, and we climbed.

"You must have been scared with three of those creepy things after you," he said after a few more flights.

"It was worse when I was trapped in an apartment with one of them," I replied without thinking about it.

"One trapped you, and you still got away unharmed? Did Ben rescue you?"

"No," I replied. "Ben didn't find me until they cornered me in an alley and I flew out."

"You flew in the human world?" He glanced at me.

"I didn't want to become their dinner. It was the only option."

I left out that it also hadn't been intentional and had been brought on by sheer panic. I didn't think he needed to know that I couldn't turn into a dragon at all. At least, not yet.

The conversation stalled until Neritas took it upon himself to point out the buildings and departments we went past in the cluster. He told me where I could go for clothing, items from the human world, food, and to work out or play games.

At no point did he mention currency, and I got the feeling it wasn't a big issue. No one was carrying a purse or wallet. It was all just dragons in human form wearing clothes and colorful dragons flying outside. When they transformed to their human state the clothes and anything they were carrying reappeared again, the magic somehow taking the objects along with them.

When we reached the registration center for the academy, Flick was waiting for me. He came forward when he saw me but frowned when he saw Neritas.

"I hope you're not bothering Scarlet," Flick told him. In his hands was a takeout box, probably for me.

"He's not. He made sure I got here safely," I replied before they could turn this into some kind of pissing contest. "Thank you, both of you, for being concerned about me."

"Looks like Flick brought you lunch too." Neritas spoke calmly but didn't look at me. Flick's eyes narrowed.

"You said you'd love a burger. So…burger." Flick held it

out, and I got the impression he wasn't so thrilled about helping me anymore.

"Thank you." The words came out more softly than I'd intended. This wasn't going well.

I frowned as he handed it over, still not looking at me.

"Right, I'm going to register." I headed toward a door to my left, an office sign above it that made me hope it was the right one. I didn't even look at what was in the food box. It could wait and I could hope they settled their differences and walked away before I came back.

Without hesitation, I pushed open the door and strode inside, pleased to see plants, sofas for those waiting, and smiling people sitting at various desks.

"You must be Scarlet," a young woman said when she spotted me. "I hoped I'd still be here when you showed up. Not everyone gets to meet a red dragon these days."

"Anyenka, be careful who you let hear you say that. Not everyone is going to take kindly to an illegal," an older woman responded. She was behind another desk in the room.

Once again I frowned. It seemed everyone already had an opinion, and they would keep talking about me as if I weren't there.

I hoped Ben found Anthony soon.

CHAPTER ELEVEN

I yawned as I woke up to my first full day in the great dragon city of Detaris. I hadn't slept much. The noise of the waves and the occasional flap of wings nearby were unfamiliar, and I'd also had a lot of weird dreams. The city felt strange. Both like a familiar home and somewhere I wasn't entirely safe.

The academy tour had been eye-opening. Thankfully, I wouldn't have to do any of the normal lessons, just the ones on the dragon world: magic, flying, and controlling my dragon powers.

And the lessons were held all over the city. To begin with, there would be plenty of time to get between them, but I'd been warned that I would be expected to fly from class to class before long.

Wanting to give myself plenty of time to find where I needed to be, I got dressed, quickly brushed my hair, and pulled on comfy boots. I was going to be doing a lot of walking before the day was done. Then I grabbed my schedule.

A lot of the dragons carried the same sort of small device the people registering me had used. I didn't have one yet, so my schedule had been printed for me, but I hoped that device was something I was going to get and be taught to use.

Before I left, I also tucked my cell phone into a pocket. It had run out of battery sometime the day before, and I'd not thought about it again or contacting my boss to update her until it was far too late. I'd not seen any electrical sockets anywhere in the entire city so far, anyway.

After taking a moment to prepare myself, I opened the door. The salty smell of the sea met my nose, and I inhaled deeply. The sun warmed my face. Once again, I was struck by how beautiful the city was, its towers stretching to the sky. It was everything I'd dreamed a magical city would be and more.

Grateful that I knew my first destination, a classroom in the thick tower beside the main academy building, I made my way toward it. I decided to explore along the way. I had plenty of time and wanted to see if I could get breakfast in a tower, too.

It was quieter this early in the day, and I hurried along. Dragons were flying already, swinging around in patterns, either practicing or patrolling. I had no way of knowing which. Since leaving the academy's registration office after my tour, I hadn't spoken to a single dragon. Not that it bothered me. I'd been grateful that Flick and Neritas were gone when I was done, but they'd kept me safe for a little while, and the burger Flick had gotten me was delicious. If nothing else, the food here was good.

As I worked out how to get to one of the restaurants

and made my way there, the city started to wake up and get busier. Again I got stares, but no one bothered me, and then Flick appeared out of nowhere.

"Sorry about yesterday," he said immediately.

"It's okay. I appreciated the food," I replied, deciding to start with honesty and see where it got me. While I didn't want Flick to think I was interested in a relationship with him, I knew I needed some people in my life here or I would be lonely. I also had a lot of questions.

"I'm going to the Ship to get some breakfast before work," he stated. "Want to join me?"

"I was heading there anyway. I think, not knowing any other restaurants yet anyway."

Flick let out a chuckle. "This place is a maze. You're going in roughly the right direction. They do the most amazing waffles."

"Perfect. I also need to figure out how to charge my cell phone before the first of my mandatory catch-up classes on all things dragon." I didn't try to hide my disdain for the schooling everyone was insisting on. I'd never enjoyed formal education.

I wasn't dumb, but rules weren't my thing. Going back to any education and following a bunch of new rules was going to take time and effort. I wasn't looking forward to learning how to live in a new society. Especially since Anthony, the only dragon I'd known for more than a few hours, was gone. I was also worried about him, and I hadn't heard from Ben.

"You have a cell phone?" Flick asked. "A human one?"

"No, I've got one the great dwarves of Khazadum made in the deep."

Flick lifted an eyebrow again, looking so quizzical that I couldn't help but laugh.

"I guess you haven't read *Lord of the Rings*."

"I have. I just didn't expect sass from an illegal unregistered."

"Well, you'd better change your expectations."

"Noted." He grinned. "Anyway, hand it over. I can charge it for you."

I reached into my pocket as he held out his hand for it, but I hesitated before handing it over. What could he do to charge it?

"It's okay. I won't muck it up. I promise."

"Fine, but if you do, let me make it clear I'll find a way to make you regret it, even if it takes me years."

"Also noted," he replied, his eyes widening a little. "I'll sleep with my door locked from now until eternity, just in case."

I chuckled and gave him the phone. Then I watched him to see what he did with it, making it obvious I was paying attention. I had expected him to pull out a charging device, but he simply put his thumb over the charging socket and concentrated.

Within a second, the screen showed the battery charging symbol. My mouth fell open when it hit a hundred percent in less than a minute or so.

"How?" I asked.

"My dragon ability. About eighteen percent of the dragons in this city can do that. Although some of them not as well."

"Good to know," I replied.

He handed me the phone and started walking toward

the restaurant again.

"I'll catch up to you," I said as I turned on the phone.

It freaked out, buzzing with all the notifications. I'd missed a lot of texts and calls.

Not only were there several from my boss, but many from my friends. And it wasn't going to be easy to explain to them what had happened to stop me from responding and from going to work.

Flick glanced between the phone and me, his jaw moving as he thought about something.

"I know you're new here, and there are probably a bunch of humans in your life, but just in case you're thinking of telling them about dragons, please don't. There's not a lot of tolerance these days for humans finding out about us. And there are rumors that you did some stuff yesterday and that's why Ben brought you in."

"Noted," I replied, saying the word the way he had.

His concerned expression changed to a grin.

"I'll order you some waffles. Three flights up, then the second bridge and another two floors."

"Got it. I'll be there before you can even consider eating mine as well."

Flick nodded and finally gave me some privacy. I didn't do anything but breathe, my mind racing as I tried to think of what to say. Stephanie was worried about me. She knew I was investigating Anthony's disappearance and that I'd found something.

I tapped out a message to her, letting her know I was safe and telling her not to worry. That I wasn't done looking, but the trail had taken me north of LA. That was all I could do for now. Before I sent the message, I added that I had a low battery and not to call because I was conserving it. Hopefully, she would believe me.

That left my boss, and I knew I would not be able to appease her. Although I wanted to send her a message and turn my phone off again, it wouldn't be professional. It wasn't like me, either. If I couldn't make it to work for any reason, I always phoned.

Given that I was supposed to avoid drawing suspicion to myself, I had to call. It took me several more seconds to summon up the courage to push the button, though.

I marveled at the signal quality as it rang. My boss picked up on the first ring, giving me no time to think about what I was going to say or get nervous about how angry she'd be.

"Scarlet, where have you been? I know this isn't like you, but I don't appreciate being left in the lurch with no idea if you're coming in or not. I gave you a job and have taken care of you for a long time. This isn't the level of courtesy I expect."

"I'm sorry, Alice. I had a family drama come up, and—"

"You don't have any family, and you already told me you were sick and had no idea when you would be back," she interrupted.

I closed my eyes. She was right, and I berated myself for not coming up with something better.

"It turns out I do have someone left. I left in a hurry and forgot my phone charger. Sorry."

"I don't buy it, Scarlet. You're not the sentimental type, and you're a lot fiercer about stuff when you're telling the truth. You can't lie for anything. Get back here for your shift tomorrow, or don't come back at all."

I gulped, knowing I'd just lost my job. There was no way I could go back to my old life and ignore all this. While I wasn't a prisoner here, I believed I would be actively discouraged from leaving before learning about the culture and the rules. I didn't want to leave, either. I wanted to learn what I could and find Anthony. He'd told me to follow the dragon, and that was what I had done. I had to see this through.

"I'm sorry. I truly am. But this is more important to me, and I can't just leave it and travel back."

"Well, you sound truthful enough about that. I won't deny that I'm disappointed in you, Scarlet. I did so much for you, and this is how you repay me. And not even a real explanation."

"I'd be there tomorrow if I could be. I understand that you'll need to find someone else. Thank you for looking out for me as much as you did. I'll hopefully get a chance to come back at some point and say goodbye properly, but that's the best I can do right now."

This seemed to soften her, but it was clear I wasn't going to have a job to go back to either way. We said goodbye, and I hung up. I turned the phone off again and took a deep breath. My heart was racing once more, the craziness and emotion of everything too much for me to cope with.

"So, you're the red who came in yesterday from an outside life," someone said from behind me.

I spun to see three girls. The one in front sported a strange, not quite human, look. She was mostly human, but in some spots, she had black scales instead of skin. Her forehead had a deep V of them, with more running across her cheekbones and the parts of her arms and legs visible below her shorts and t-shirt.

The two girls on either side of her had green scales, and their faces were almost entirely covered. While I'd realized that the shapeshifting was somehow controlled by each dragon, it had not occurred to me that there might be something in between. That the appearance a dragon could take was fluid.

"I'm the red that came in yesterday," I confirmed, hoping this wouldn't take long. After the phone call to my former boss, I didn't have much patience.

"You should go back to whatever hovel you were living in before one of us rescued you."

"Can't do that. Got stuff to do, things to learn, and places to be. I'll be sure to tell the teacher in my first class that…" I paused, hoping she'd realize I was asking for her name.

"She's Lindsay," the green dragon on the left said.

"Then I'll be sure to tell my teacher at my first class that Lindsay thinks her opinion that a dragon she's never met before should leave is more important than me working with Ben and others to find a missing dragon who is being hunted by at least three shadow catchers."

The green dragons gasped, and I had to fight not to roll my eyes at how easy it was to manipulate them. I was getting sick of having to defend myself or be on my guard, however, and I was pretty sure Lindsay didn't appreciate the sass.

She folded her arms even tighter and jutted out her jaw as she eyed me up and down.

"You might be a red dragon, but they're not special

anymore, if any of them ever were. The delusions of grandeur make sense, though."

"So I've heard, but don't worry, I have no aspirations to any throne. I just want to find a missing dragon and learn what I need to do to keep your leaders happy. Then I'll go back to my hovel. Now, if you'll excuse me, someone is holding breakfast for me, and I don't want to add being rude to the crime of daring to be red."

I walked toward the next set of steps and ascended without looking back. Although I half-expected someone to yell at me to stop, no one did.

I soon found my way to the Ship, where Flick was waiting with two piles of waffles in front of him.

"I was thinking of eating both these plates. Perfect timing," he said as my chair moved out on its own.

Trying not to react to the trick even though it was cool, I sat and focused on the stack of food in front of me. If nothing else, I'd eat well while I was here.

CHAPTER TWELVE

More than a little over my lessons for the day, I sighed and picked up my notebook. So far, I'd sat through a class on dragon and human history and another on how to avoid being detected—a lesson that amounted to nothing more than "stay in human form and don't use magic unless you're in the city." All of it was emphasized by pointless and unrealistic scenario after pointless, unrealistic scenario.

My final lesson of the morning was flight for beginners. I assumed that in a class that was starting at the beginning, I was going to be surrounded by very young dragons. The other classes had dragons of mixed ages, although I'd been the oldest in both classes. And the only red dragon.

Throughout the day, I picked up on the vibe that there was more to being a red dragon than I had been told. Ben had mentioned that some had been royalty and others had done questionable crap in the past. I wanted to find out what my ancestors had been up to. And I didn't doubt for a second that I was related to the ones who had done stuff they shouldn't. Probably awful exiles or something.

I'd also come to terms early with not knowing who my parents were, and I didn't have any new hope that I would find out now. A part of me had always known they weren't alive anymore, whoever they were. And coming here hadn't changed that.

What *had* changed was my belief in the future I could have. I had not been made welcome here, but I was filled with a strange hope and a coming home sort of feeling. It had been bizarre and there was a steep learning curve to the society here, but I still felt as if I were in the right place for the first time in my life. It wasn't going to be easy to adjust, though.

With that in mind, I was eager to make my way to one of the most oddly shaped towers in the city. This one started as an oval at the base and shifted into a tall, thin rectangle.

A couple of floors from the top, I paused, grateful I'd started this journey from a high floor already. My legs were killing me, and I had begun feeling a sway to the tower that was disconcerting.

As I'd suspected and feared, the other dragons walking up this high with me were young and all in human form. Apparently, dragons learned to fly a lot like birds. You just jumped and figured it out on the way down.

The top of the tower had a dragon-sized diving board over the ocean. This wasn't going to be as dull as my other classes had been.

The teacher was one of the oldest dragons I'd seen so far, with a bushy white beard and a smile that lit up the center of it. He had a shock of wavy white hair to match, making me think of a dragon equivalent of Santa Claus.

The young dragons were nervous. Most of them looked to be about ten in human years. It didn't help me feel any calmer. As I was the oldest one, there was a good chance I would be asked to lead.

"Okay. I say this every first lesson, and there's a good reason for that." The teacher got up from his chair. His voice was gentle but still loud enough to cut through the young dragons' animated chatter. "You're all nervous, even the ones of you who don't look it."

His eyes flicked to me briefly as he said the last words and for a moment it was as if someone was looking into the very depths of my soul and time stood still. I felt both seen and vulnerable.

It passed as quickly as it started, but I was calmer for it. I wasn't the only one who benefited; everyone settled in to listen.

"You're dragons, born to rule the skies and fly with grace and strength. Each of you has that built into your body. It's instinctive. The nerves you feel are your minds asking questions. It's natural too, but don't question the essence of who you are. You can fly. Every one of you has the capacity. All you have to do is embrace the natural and let your body do what it already knows. And then I get to be the laziest teacher in this city."

Many of them laughed at the final sentence, then a younger boy stepped forward.

"I'll go first," he said, making a few others gasp.

Our teacher nodded and the kid moved forward, morphing into a dragon as soon as he was clear of the group. He moved to the diving board, which brought him out across the water and to the edge of the city.

I held my breath while I watched and waited for him to do something. The seconds dragged by, and I wondered if the kid had frozen, but then he stepped off.

Almost immediately, he dropped and everyone leaned forward to watch what happened. My stomach knotted. I half expected him to hit the water.

Instead, about halfway down, his wings opened and caught the wind. He soared forward, slowing his descent as he began to glide.

The class collectively sighed in relief as the kid figured out how to flap and rose. Within seconds, he wheeled around the tower and climbed up into the sky above us.

Switching focus from him to the rest of us, the teacher encouraged the next dragon forward.

From here the teacher chose the kids one by one, suggesting some of the braver, more competent dragons go first. Everyone succeeded, and those left on the top grew bolder as time went by. I was amazed by how well the strategy was working.

That said, near the middle he picked out a shaking kid who struggled to take dragon form and kept morphing partway to blue scales before returning to human form. When this happened for a third time, the teacher came forward and whispered something. Eventually, he held his dragon shape. The rest of the class encouraged him to step off, but he hesitated for quite some time.

In the end, he either fell off or someone pushed him; I couldn't see which. He plummeted so fast that we all gasped as one.

My eyes went wide as he kept dropping. The water below looked ominous, as if it might swallow him whole.

Ten yards from the bottom of the tower, a large black dragon swooped out from somewhere, came up underneath the kid, and caught him. They flew forward together as another dragon swept down and flew ahead of them. They tossed the kid between them, forcing him to get used to being in the air.

No one said a word as we watched, relieved but also stunned. The two dragons didn't let up, bouncing the boy between them until he got used to it and spread his wings out.

I exhaled as he supported himself for the first time and neither dragon had to catch him anymore. The entire class relaxed.

"Some of you will need a little more help. That's okay too," the teacher said with a knowing grin.

Fighting back a laugh, I relaxed too. I still had one nagging doubt, though. The two black dragons below were strong enough to catch the kids who fell, but could they catch a full-grown red dragon?

There was no way to know but I was sure I was about to find out.

Despite my fears, I kept my thoughts to myself and my outward appearance calm, a look long schooled into me by life. If people didn't get a reaction, they left you alone. I could wear that mask with ease.

I continued to wait as the teacher ushered every single other dragon forward, getting them into the air and flying one by one. I was pretty sure I'd been standing on the roof for over an hour by the time I was the last one left. The rest had landed on the nearby towers and changed back to human form or were still flying around the city.

Eager to begin now that it was my turn, I stepped back, considering trying to change into dragon form. Before I could, the teacher came forward again and tilted his head back to look up at the majority of his students, all of them hovering in the air or sitting on the edge of the platform that constituted the top of the tower.

"Well done, all of you. Next lesson, we'll go over control and technique, but most of you have the hang of this. Keep practicing—but go somewhere else, if you please."

I frowned, taking a couple of steps back toward the edge. Was I not going to have the chance to fly?

"What about me?" I asked, feeling all my pent-up stress and confusion since arriving come out with my words and bundle into one angry question.

The teacher didn't respond to my emotional outburst, but he did turn to face me and studied me for a second.

"I understand you're a recent addition to the city."

"Yes. And not entirely happily. I want to find a friend more than I want to be here."

"Anthony?"

"Yes. He lived near me, but something happened to him."

"And I understand you flew while being hunted there."

"Sort of."

"One of those situations where it happened because you needed to, and instinct took over?" He looked thoughtful.

"Something like that. I turned back into a human as soon as I hit the deck."

"That isn't why I dismissed the rest of the class. Please

don't feel it is a slight on you or a lack of faith in your ability. I understand you are also a red dragon?"

"Yes, something that seems to either piss people off or make them want to suck up to me."

"Exactly, and you're about to reveal that nature to everyone here. I thought it best that you did so while fewer eyes were watching. It's lunchtime, and while there are still dragons in the air, there are not as many right now."

I started to relax at this explanation. It made sense. He wasn't only being understanding, but he had some kind of plan and had also thought about what was best for me.

"You have the famous red dragon fire. I must say that it's an honor to be the teacher standing here right now. I'd like to fly with you if that's okay."

"In case I'm so heavy that those two down there can't catch me?" I asked.

He chuckled.

"I honestly don't think you'll need any of us, but I won't deny that it had occurred to me. Consider this simply an offer to be there, no matter what happens. I am your teacher, and this way, I can offer you the safest environment in which to learn."

"Thank you. Although it sounds like I do better with not being safe when it comes to embracing my true form."

Again he chuckled, and I liked the sound. It was a deep rumble that spoke of years of mirth. And it had done something nothing else had. Calm me.

Feeling far braver, I walked to the edge in human form and tried to focus. I had no idea how to take dragon form, and nothing happened for so long that I started to feel awkward.

"Close your eyes and think about the moment you turned last time. Or the first time, if it's happened more than once," the teacher said. He was also still in human form.

I wasn't going to argue with my own teacher so I closed my eyes and thought about being trapped in the alley. At first, I hadn't known I'd changed, but I had realized as I'd flown and heard a voice in my head. Only now did I remember that it had been Ben's voice. He'd somehow communicated with me.

There you are, another voice said in my head. *Pause there for a moment.*

Although I wanted to open my eyes, I didn't. I felt the wind blowing over skin that felt different.

Feel it. Get used to the difference. Get used to how you fit like this, then slowly move forward when you're ready.

Having a calm voice in my head made all the difference. First, I concentrated on breathing, feeling my much larger lungs inflate and deflate, my scaled torso moving with them. I lifted my legs and arms one by one and flexed my claws. While I was doing this, I accidentally swished my tail.

I felt my teacher's amusement when I tested everything a second time. Finally, I opened my eyes and watched my red-scaled body parts as they moved. It was strange to see this new body. It felt both right and unfamiliar, but there was something liberating about it. As if this was more natural and I had always been in this form. But there was also something foreign about it, like I didn't know how wide or how strong I was.

Not sure what to do next, I tried unfurling my wings and at least making sure I knew what that felt like.

The teacher had turned into a white dragon beside me. I stretched out the wing nearest to him, and he hunkered down to let it go over his head. After doing this several times, there was nothing else I could do to prep. If I was going to fly, I needed to make the leap.

I jumped before he could stop me. At first, my mind froze. I wanted to become human again. Panic tightened my chest as I fell, but I felt Ben enter my mind.

You okay? he asked, his mental voice pitched higher than normal as if he felt my fear too.

Just learning to fly, I thought, not sure that my response could be heard.

Spreading your wings might help. The amusement in Ben's voice took me by surprise, but it also snapped me out of the brain fog and helped me do just that.

The wind caught underneath them, and I swooped forward and out to sea, two black dragons and a white coming with me. Thinking back to how I had collided with a building the first time I'd flown, I was already grateful for the lack of them ahead now. It had felt odd to flap my wings to get higher, and even odder to feel objects give way beneath my scales.

I flapped, thinking only about the rush of air on my face and how beautiful the water looked with the sun glinting off it.

You need to turn soon, or you'll leave the protected area, the teacher said.

Although it shouldn't have surprised me, I froze again. I didn't feel able to turn.

Somehow, I did, however, and I was soon heading back to the city. I played and changed altitude as I flew, and it felt wonderful.

Thank you, I thought, feeling free in a way I never had before. This was what I was meant to be. *Thank you for everything.*

CHAPTER THIRTEEN

For several beautiful minutes I felt as if everything was right in my world. I was flying on the edges of the city, with two black dragons and my teacher staying with me.

It was perfect.

Until several dragons appeared from nowhere and cut me off. I banked quickly and tried to rise out of their way, but a tower was so close I clipped it with a wing. Pain flared, and then another dragon came across me, forcing me to turn again.

Fly up and back to the lesson tower, my teacher said to me, his voice sounding agitated for the first time.

There was no way I was going to argue as he and the black dragons came closer, their wings almost touching mine as I ascended. No more dragons intercepted me, thankfully.

I landed on the tower's top too quickly for it to be graceful and slid a few meters. I exhaled and shifted back to human form. The two black dragons didn't land, swooping across and then forming a rotating sort of defense around the top of the tower. It was comforting to know I was protected, and I felt compelled to thank them, although I didn't know the names of either dragon or what they looked like in human form.

"Sorry," my teacher said after resuming human form. "As I said, reactions to red dragons can be..."

"Extreme," I said for him.

He nodded, looking sad.

"Thank you for doing everything you could to mitigate it."

"You're welcome. Just so you're aware, you're safe when you're close to or on the top of this tower. Even with the antics they're willing to pull."

I blinked, wondering if he had that much power and what it was about this tower, but I didn't get a chance to ask.

"I have another class to teach in a couple of minutes, and you should get lunch after everything you've done. I look forward to seeing you again soon. It will get easier. I know it doesn't seem that way, but it will."

"Thank you..." My voice trailed off. I didn't know his name despite the lesson.

"Scarlet, isn't it? Call me Jared. If you ever need anything outside teaching hours, head to the lower east side of the tower, the part that looks like someone stacked a bunch of eggs on top of each other."

I smiled at the description, having noticed the area earlier. Each egg had a different-colored sheen. I could see why someone might want to live there. Not that I'd had any choice about my residence, but that was a concern for another day.

The sheer number of dragons hovering nearby made it clear I wasn't welcome. It was time to retreat and find somewhere safer. But where to go was the big question.

I'd heard Ben in my head while I was in dragon form, and the library was only a couple of towers away, so I opted to go see him. Maybe with the journal I carried and whatever research he had been able to do in the last day or so there would lead us to Anthony.

Fear gnawed at the base of my spine as I descended the first flight of stairs and started my journey. A teenager came up soon after, taking me by surprise. As I hurried past him, I was careful not to meet his gaze. I didn't want to be recognized or stopped.

That was the worst part about the city—the numerous flights of stairs and not knowing what lingered around every corner. Not knowing if the next dragon I met would be friendly or an enemy.

I also kept getting turned around. Figuring out where the bridges were and what was on each floor was a nightmare. The city was like a maze. A huge, complicated maze, and I was one of the mice scurrying through it to my next destination.

My stomach grumbled, reminding me that it was lunchtime. I was supposed to take care of my body, but as I headed to the next flight of stairs, I heard someone land in the doorway behind me.

I heard their footsteps hurry after me, but I sped up, taking steps two at a time with one hand outstretched to keep pushing me around the tower. The tactic helped me stay far enough ahead that they couldn't reach me. I didn't slow on the next landing, thinking that I needed to go down one more set of steps before taking a bridge, heading back up a floor, and then crossing to the library tower.

I would be coming into the library from a high point, and I had no idea if that was allowed or if there was some etiquette or convention I had to follow. I didn't know where Ben would be, but there was a reason that the nerds at school had always spent their time in the library. It was a safe zone. I hoped dragon culture had equally fierce librarians who valued their quiet over anything else.

As I reached the next floor, however, two more dragons were waiting for me in human form, arms crossed. They were blocking both doors.

"Excuse me. I'm in a hurry. Ben has called me to the library," I said, only sort of lying.

Neither person moved, and I slowed to try to remember which exit I wanted. With nowhere to go unless I pushed past them, I was forced to stop and weigh my options.

At the same time the booted feet were still thundering down the stairs.

If I waited much longer, I would be sandwiched between the ones that were blocking my way and my unknown pursuer. I preferred being rude, even if I had to apologize later, to getting caught in the middle of a group of bullies intent on putting me in my place. Whatever that was supposed to be.

"I really must insist. I need to get to the library. It's urgent. A man's life could be at stake."

Now I was lying. But when it came to saving my own skin, it was for a good cause. Neither of them moved, so I rushed toward the right-hand one, hoping it was the right direction. The dragon was surprised, and I slipped past him as he danced in a circle to grab me.

His fingers caught on the edge of my sweatshirt but slid off. It slowed me down a little and threw me off balance as I hurried away. This bridge was made of wooden slats that shook and swayed, so I didn't get my balance back as I crossed it.

Thankfully, I made it into the other tower, but no sooner had I put my foot on the first step than the two green dragons and black dragon girls from before came through the door on the opposite side. The grin on the black dragon's face told me everything I needed to know. She wanted to be the one to catch me, and I would not like how that turned out.

I darted to my left to climb the steps, not sure what else I could do to avoid them. It was broad daylight, and everyone knew the city far better than I did, so the odds of getting away weren't in my favor.

Still, I took the stairs two at a time, not willing to give up until there was truly no way out. My flight made the others bolder, and they shouted as they ran after me. I hadn't wanted to run from them, but there were so many that staying to fight wasn't an option. Not this time.

Another three dragons stood in the way on the next floor, all three of them ready to catch me.

There was only one option. I would have to barrel through them.

Having a bunch of people bothering me simply because of the color of my scales was starting to piss me off. I hadn't chosen to be a dragon, let alone a red dragon. And I still had no idea what was so bad about being red.

"Get out of my way," I bellowed.

Their eyes went wider, clearly not expecting me to be fierce, but I was beyond caring. I didn't want to be seen or noticed. I just wanted to be left alone so I could go to the dragon who was looking for my friend.

No sooner had I thought this than pitch-black darkness filled the tower. I heard swearing as everyone else went still. Practiced at moving silently in the dark to avoid detection in foster homes, I moved to the side as quickly as I could without making a sound.

Someone moved close to me, aiming for where I'd been, but they missed and crashed into another dragon at the top of the stairs.

I ignored my heart as it hammered in my chest and the fear at the base of my spine, and instead, moved closer to the exit.

I didn't know if the three dragons in my path had moved, so I did the most logical thing I could think of and moved to the edge of the room and went in the opposite direction to where I wanted to go. I remembered another door and another bridge I could escape through while they tripped over each other in the dark.

Of course, it was also dark outside. When I reached the bridge, I felt around to grab a rail on one side, taking a couple of seconds to find it. They delay had me on edge, but it was better than being caught. I stepped out onto the bridge and out of the midst of the other dragons.

For the first time in a while, I could think. The chaos was behind me, and the area I was in was wrapped in darkness—a safe zone of sorts—and it was helping. This wasn't the first time darkness had descended on me during a terrifying moment.

Although I wasn't sure how, the darkness was an element that I was creating. In much the same way that the shift into dragon form and the subsequent flight had happened when I needed it, so had this. And if that was true, then I could control the darkness.

With this in mind, I focused on keeping the tower dark while having it get lighter where I was and ahead of me.

Nothing happened at first, but then the area around me grew a little brighter. The sounds of chaos continued behind me as more dragons got caught up in the darkness, some of them innocent bystanders who were just trying to get through the tower.

I stepped to the edge of the bridge to get a good look at the rest of the route, but I'd screwed myself. This bridge led to a tower that only connected to the library at the bottom. And I wasn't going to last if I had to go down that far only to come back up again to get to the library.

Pausing, I tried to work out how many people were in the small tower behind me, but they were beginning to adjust to the darkness and work together. I would never sneak through the building and past them all now. That left only one option—I would have to fly up from this bridge and around the tower to the library. But the bridge wasn't wide enough to accommodate a dragon, and I hadn't practiced transforming as I landed. It was a scary thought.

I thought about what Jared had said. About fear and pressure sometimes making things easier to attempt. I hoped he was right, because I was terrified, and a lot was riding on me getting to the library and Ben.

With no other option, I concentrated for a moment, then launched off the side of the bridge with my eyes closed. I fell as someone yelled from the tower doorway. I'd been spotted.

I imagined transforming, trying to channel everything as I had earlier, but my body already knew what I needed. By the time I'd called up my first memory of being a dragon, my wings were already outstretched and I was flying.

My stomach lurched as I powered up and forward before banking to turn around the tower as swiftly as I could. As my wings went down for the third time, I heard the roar of another dragon, and a shadow came across me.

The second that I could see the bridge and entrance to the library tower I powered forward, tucking my head down and thrusting my legs back to streamline my body. I was terrified that I was going to crash into the large building and break it the way I had the first time I'd flown.

Scarlet? Ben asked. *What are you doing?*

Making a birthday cake. What does it feel like I'm doing?

The entrance was coming up fast. I closed my eyes and focused on turning back into a human before I hit it. I opened them a second later. It was just in time to see the library as my body caught the side of the doorway hard enough to spin me. My momentum carried me the rest of the way through, however.

I landed awkwardly, twisting my leg before going down hard on my side. When I stopped moving, I was several feet into the room, facing the door. My right side was on fire from hitting the floor, and my left shoulder hurt from catching the doorway. The tower was remarkably unscathed.

Another dragon landed in the doorway, taking human form as he did. It was one of the males who had blocked my path earlier. I shuffled back and bumped into a bookshelf so hard that most of the books fell on top of me.

"What's going on here?" a woman yelled as she came closer.

I exhaled with relief, hoping that this meant my ordeal was finally over. More dragons landed behind the guy but they looked wary and kept their distance.

"I'm sorry. I am still learning to fly," I said as I got to my feet. I locked eyes with the people chasing me, daring them to contradict me and confess. I knew they wouldn't. But there was a sort of honor currency being exchanged now. My lack of accusation, and acceptance of all the blame for disturbing the library meant they owed me. The question was, would any of them honor it? Would they feel like they were in my debt, at least for a short while?

When I got to my feet, the librarian was standing in the middle of the room, surveying the damage.

Once again, I apologized, but I didn't look away from the dragons by the door. With every passing second more of them landed.

"Is everything all right?" she asked, peering at me before looking very pointedly at the aggressive group outside.

"It's fine now. They were just making sure I didn't break the tower when I hit it."

The woman's mouth became a flat line, almost as if she disapproved of the lie, but if she had a problem with my words, she decided to accept them anyway.

"All right, well, you're here now. Anyone who doesn't need to be in this section of the library should go." She lifted her head just a fraction higher, making it clear no one should argue.

To my relief, this worked. The dragons outside left, flying off one by one.

I deflated. Somehow I'd outrun, out-magicked, and outflown over ten other dragons. And it was only my first day in the dragon city, plus I had no idea what I was doing.

CHAPTER FOURTEEN

"Now, are you going to tell me why you're here?" the librarian asked when we were alone.

"I'm looking for Ben. I want to help him find Anthony, and he said I could help with his research." Although that was the truth, the librarian frowned as she picked up a book from the floor.

"What is your name? I haven't seen you up here before."

"Scarlet."

"Ah. You're the new dragon who caused all the havoc in LA two days ago. Do you know how difficult that was to put right? You made a dent in a popular park in one of the busiest cities in the world."

I gritted my teeth, not liking how this conversation had started. None of that had been deliberate, and I had only done as much as was needed to save my life.

"I'm sure it wasn't easy to put right," I replied when she took the book from me and bent to pick up another of the ones I'd knocked onto the floor. "But I'm grateful that it was. However, that's not why I'm here. All that happened while I was trying to figure out where Anthony is."

For a moment the fierce woman didn't speak, picking up books as I stooped to get another. She gently tucked them back onto the shelves as quickly as I could collect them, knowing where they went with a glance at each title alone.

"You'd best be gone," she said when there were only a few left to put away. "I can do the rest, and these aren't the sort of books you should be seeing or reading. These are some of the most important books the library owns, and the information is sensitive."

"I can't leave," I replied, fetching another book from the floor in a slower manner. "I really do need to see Ben. He asked me to come and find him as soon as I could, so here I am. Ready to help him."

"Ben knows trainees aren't allowed in the main area of the library for their first week and in the upper levels for several months."

"That may be true, but he did ask me to come here and told me that you could talk to him if you had a problem with it." I shrugged, trying to take some of the frustration out of my body language and show that I was just trying to do as I was asked as well.

"Ben doesn't make the rules. I do. This is not a suitable area for someone who doesn't understand our ways, and definitely not for someone so...reckless."

"I'm pretty sure Anthony, who is out there somewhere being hunted by at least three shadow catchers, doesn't care about your rules right now. I can help him, and Ben knows that. I need to see him. Now!" My temper flared, and I clenched my fists and set my jaw. For now, the books were forgotten.

The librarian didn't budge.

"This is a quiet space that deserves respect and care. You clearly aren't ready to be here. I should have known a red dragon wouldn't understand, respect or follow the rules." The librarian puffed out her chest and lifted her chin as if I'd just threatened her very existence.

I sighed, not sure what I was going to do, other than fly outside again and try to get Ben to come down or out of wherever he was hiding.

Ready to leave, and not wanting to argue anymore, I grabbed the bag I'd shoved my stuff into. It had gone flying when I'd landed. The journal had also slid out, so I quickly tucked it back inside.

"Wait," the librarian said, coming over to me. "I can't let you take a book. I saw that."

"I've not taken a book. It was mine already."

"And I wasn't born yesterday. Hand it over."

"No. It's not one of your books. I'm supposed to take it to Ben, but if you won't let me through, I can't do that."

I started to walk away, but she grabbed my arm.

"Enough, young lady. This is not the way adult dragons behave, and I won't hesitate to call a guard to get that book back. Typical behavior for a red dragon. Acting like this won't get you anywhere." The librarian's grip was like a vise, however, and she was calling for the guard in a high-pitched shout. She followed it with an ear-piercing whistle that made me wince.

My frustration built and made it even harder to stay calm. I was exhausted as well as tired of everyone judging me without knowing me. However, Ben had asked me to keep the journal a secret, and I needed the safety that he represented right now.

There was nothing I could do but try to prove my point. I reached into my bag and pulled the book out as one of the black dragons from earlier came through the door I was facing, transforming as he did. He shifted with so much grace that it made my spectacular entry look even more out of control than it had been.

As the librarian went to take the journal, I yanked it out of her reach.

"This isn't your book, and if you give me a couple of seconds, I will prove it to you," I said, trying to sound far calmer than I felt.

The guard looked between us both, then came over with a hand out.

"I don't know what's going on here, but it seems to be about that book. I think we should calm down a little and sort this out with some dignity and grace, don't you both?"

"That sounds wonderful," I replied.

He reached over to encourage the librarian to let go of my arm. She scowled but did so and stepped back a little.

"I've come here to find Ben." I looked at the guard, desperately hoping he could sort it out.

"No, you've come here to try to take a book." The librarian glared at me. "Probably on some kind of dare from all those dragons outside."

I clenched the fist not holding the book again, having to fight to stay calm once more.

"I think it might be a good idea for me to take the

book." The guard reached out to take it. "We can see who it belongs to and if it doesn't—"

"I can't give you the book," I interrupted. "I was instructed to keep it safe. There's a letter on the first page that is addressed to me, and it explains why I have it."

The guard didn't look pleased. "You're in a safe place here. I really must insist."

"No. You won't," Ben said, his voice coming from behind me and off to one side.

Everyone looked his way as he came forward, taking a few more steps through a now-open door.

"Scarlet is telling the truth. She is here to see me and aid me in my research, and I assume she informed you of that. The book she is holding is not for everyone to see or read but pertains to a very delicate matter regarding Anthony's disappearance. He entrusted the book to her, so it is hers to do with as she wishes."

The librarian gaped, then narrowed her eyes at me. I avoided her look, not wanting to focus on anything but Ben. After giving him a nod, I moved in his direction. No one stopped me.

"I don't like this. It's irresponsible at best for you to let someone foreign to our ways into the most heavily guarded section of our library." The librarian stepped closer, her body quivering with barely controlled anger.

The guard didn't move, clearly not sure what he was meant to do now. I got the impression that Ben had a level of authority that made the guard unsure if he should be contradicted.

"That may be true," Ben said, entirely focused on the librarian. "But in this case, Scarlet is far more concerned for Anthony than any of us. He was acting as a father to her. He kept her safe, and our way of life along with it. He's entrusted her with information that only she knows and the journal she carries. It is his wishes that it stays with her."

"And this is my library, and it is entrusted to me. On top of that, he isn't here to make his feelings known, so I can only go on mine."

"That's not true," I replied, opening the book.

The first page became visible as I picked up the letter and moved to open the envelope. A gasp made me look at the librarian. Her hand covered her mouth as she stared at the writing on the first page.

"Is that..."? Her voice trailed off.

"Yes, it is," Ben replied. I had no idea what they meant

Despite this already appearing to do something to help, I pulled the letter out of the envelope and handed it over. This time she took it almost respectfully and read it.

No one spoke, everyone waiting for her to announce her verdict on what was going on and if she believed it. Finally, she gave the letter back.

"I wish you had mentioned this sooner," she stated. "This makes what Anthony intended very clear."

I raised my eyebrows, not appreciating having this put on me. I'd spent the last few minutes doing exactly that.

"I told you I had a letter from him. I can't possibly know who is trustworthy and who isn't. I just want to get Anthony back. Since I got here, I've had people judging me for the color of my scales. I don't know what my ancestors did, but I'm not them. I'm barely a dragon at all. The only dragon I have known my whole life is

Anthony, and I didn't even know that's what he was two days ago. Now, please, let me help Ben so we can find him."

The ensuing silence was heavy and full of tension as I'd called attention to their prejudices. After a few seconds, the librarian took a step back and looked at the guard.

"You may go. Thank you."

"That's fine with me. I don't like books anywhere near that much, and I don't want to stand between two women having an argument over a guy." The guard grinned, shot me a wink, and practically fell backwards out of the doorway behind him. He turned into a dragon and launched up and outward.

For the second time I marveled at the level of control he had, but I only allowed myself the briefest of seconds to watch.

"Shall we?" Ben said, motioning for me to join him through the door.

I didn't hesitate, putting the journal and the letter back in my bag as I hurried over to him. There was no way I would get an apology from the librarian, and I wasn't going to demand one. It wouldn't be worth the effort.

Ben led me through the interior door and shut it behind us. Beyond was a small room and a set of stairs that led up. It was dim, illuminated only by a small lantern on a table. Ben picked it up and motioned for me to follow him up the stairs.

Feeling a sense of trepidation, I climbed beside him and looked out on what appeared to be an impossible area. It was a huge chamber full of books from floor to ceiling that shouldn't have fit inside the tower.

"Welcome to one of the best-kept secrets in this city," Ben said.

"I think I understand better why she was so difficult about letting me in," I replied as I walked down one of the aisles. It was the most amazing sight I had ever seen and I knew I was staring like a child in a wonderland.

The shelves were a rich chestnut-brown color and shone with polish and care. They stretched so high that each had a ladder wrought from the same wood on runners. The books were all leather-bound, but they weren't identical. The leather was dyed in many hues that made the place a wash of variety.

"Well, as much as I would love to give you a tour and let you look at all the books you wish to, I believe I have found something that will help us translate that journal of yours. With any luck, we can figure out what Anthony was trying to tell you and if we can help him."

I wasn't going to argue. As much as I wanted to explore, it sounded as if there would be time for that after we found Anthony. I was worried about him right now. I'd only been holding back and going to lessons because there was nothing else I could do.

Ben led me down another aisle with shelves higher than the eye could see, and we came to another small table with another lamp sitting on it. It seemed to get brighter as we approached. He added a second one to make the area even brighter.

There was a chair in front of several open books and another to one side. I took the second chair and pulled out the journal again.

"So, why did everyone freak out when they saw this?" I asked, opening it to the first page.

"Because it's written in a language that only the royal bloodline and the secret protectors of the royal bloodline were meant to know. Plus a few others."

"So, Anthony was involved with royalty? Or does that make me royalty, or both?" The questions tumbled out as I thought of them and then I blushed.

"Maybe neither, and even if it did mean those things, you don't want everyone to know. Trust me."

"What does it mean if *not* either of those?" I asked, hoping an alternative was more likely.

"That this needed to be kept secret, and he was willing to use a language that could get him into trouble to make sure you and very few others could follow him and work out what he was trying to do, and figure out what drew the attention of the shadow catchers."

I nodded, but I still had so many questions. However, If we were to help Anthony, they would have to wait.

"Here's the kicker with this language. He didn't just write it in another language that's hard to translate. He also wrote it in code. And each page has a different code word to unlock the meaning. That is typical of the language as well."

"Sort of like a secret within a secret."

"Exactly. Which means that even though I found books to help translate this into English, only you can translate it."

"Great," I replied, feeling anything but. It seemed Anthony had forgotten I didn't enjoy this sort of thing. "Where do I begin?"

"I was hoping you'd tell me. Usually, things like this have a code phrase. Something that's said between the two people that no one else would guess or know. Like the words in a book or a poem. It would be something he'd expect you to think of."

Exhaling, I ran a hand through my hair and thought. This wasn't going to be easy. I had no idea where to begin. Anthony had taught me to play board games. And he'd been in my life for a while, but we rarely talked about books and never poetry. We didn't like the same kind of movies. Whatever we had in common, nothing came to mind. I didn't know what Anthony might have used.

This was going to be a nightmare.

CHAPTER FIFTEEN

"Okay, not Scarlet, then," I said over an hour later. We'd tried a dozen words, but each had returned a paragraph of gibberish. Nothing we could work with.

"What about 'board?' For board games."

"It's unlikely since you wouldn't have anything to follow it with, but at this point it seems any guess is as good as another." Ben was frustrated, and his short hair was sticking up all over his head in tufts where he had put his hand in and tugged on it.

Feeling incredibly similar myself, I helped him figure out what the words would translate to if "board" was our keyword. We only needed five words to know it was another dead end.

I leaned back. My body ached from sitting in one place for so long. This was the worst process I had ever gone through. I just wanted to find Anthony and talk to him. So many people had been judging me, I'd lost my job, and despite the awesomeness of finding out I was a badass dragon and could fly, I would have given anything to go back to my previous life.

I would have gone to his apartment on a day like today with some kind of offering like steaks from the butcher's or a takeout meal. I would have poured my heart out to him. As I thought about that I felt the first tears sting my eyes and threaten to fall.

"Hey, there's no need for that. We'll work this out, don't worry. And Anthony will be fine while we look for him. I know I've said this before, but he's a very capable dragon. We'll find him."

Although I nodded, more tears came. Ben wasn't Anthony, and it only helped so much to hear those things. I wanted to be in Anthony's living room, but as I imagined being there, something flicked on in my head.

"Cotton." I wiped the tears away. "Try, 'Cotton Candy, do we need to get some?'"

Ben's eyes went wide, but he nodded and grabbed a fresh sheet of paper. Within a minute, it was clear that I'd finally found the right word to begin.

Finally, the journal was going to make sense.

I did everything I could to help, beginning to get the idea of how to translate the journal entry until we had our first page.

This is the beginning of what I hope will be a short account. But, in case things don't go the way I want, I've written this in a way that I hope will one day lead another on to the right path. And because of who I am, it will also contain some random thoughts and feelings. I never could journal about anything without expressing a little of who I am on the page.

Today I met her. Scarlet. She wasn't what I expected. All legs and innocence and seemingly none of the hotheadedness red dragons are known for. She was so alone she broke my heart, however. Sitting in the hallway with no key, no food, and almost no other belongings, clutching a bucket of cotton candy like it was a lifeline.

Protecting her while not letting her know who she truly is will not be an easy task. And it's not one I take on with any great grace. I believe it's the right thing to do. There is, of course, a good chance that this will all be for nothing, and both I and my patron could be completely wrong. I may have to face that someday. If there is even a small chance that we are right, however, I must do it, and this is the best way to do so.

Now that I have her situated nearby and she can live a normal life, I can focus on the main part of my task, which is finding out what all this means and if anything can be done in time. And yes, dear reader of this journal in the future, I know I am being vague. I've never been the sort of person to put forth my theories, but present them in various ways and under various guarded words. Simply because I don't want to allow my own internal bias to change yours.

The wonderful thing about theories is that they explore what might come to be. But if I suggest a possibility to another, I may skew my reader's imaginings of other possibilities and make it less likely that their different set of biases could challenge mine and change the theory for the better. That said, I will recount here what I find out and what it could mean with as little bias as I can.

I will also be establishing a safe house, or possibly two, and a backup copy of this journal. Or three. And anything else I think will be useful. Some of my plans would likely fall apart if another dragon were to realize what I'm up to. The other adver-

sary I might face, I won't mention yet. If they realize what I'm doing, or trying to do, all may be lost.

The dragon community has become complacent, and I can only be sorry for playing a part in not stopping it. It has allowed the old enemy to scheme against us, and if we're not careful, our kingdom and all those we protect will fall.

Swallowing nervously, I glanced at Ben. Out of all the words, I only understood two important points. First, Anthony had been protecting me from something, and second, he had contingencies and safe houses.

"What did you say the next word will be?" Ben asked me, his voice more serious than ever.

"Candy. It's what he called me sometimes. 'Cotton Candy.'"

"Okay. Don't tell anyone else, ever again. Do you understand?"

For a moment I was too stunned to speak, but eventually, I nodded. I felt rooted to the chair with fear, my body frozen, my heart pounding so hard I could hear the rush of blood past my ears. Yet my breathing remained calm, shallow, and steady, absorbing my focus.

If there was an enemy and Anthony had been worried about them before he had disappeared, then I'd been chased by some strange creature, did that mean he was dead? Or was he still trying to protect me? If his journal was meant to reassure me, it was having the opposite effect.

It was some time later when I snapped back to reality and found that Ben had translated several more pages using the words I gave him, each one coming out of my mouth as if another had spoken them.

The translated journal told me that Anthony had inserted himself into my life with intention, and I felt betrayed. I'd thought I had chosen him. That it was something unexpected and therefore strangely safer, but I had been manipulated.

Despite that feeling, it also told me that he cared. Every paragraph oozed with concern and a paternal feeling toward me. It also contained a genuine desire to make sure I didn't face the world alone anymore.

At first, I despaired that we would find him, his thoughts almost rambling, but when we reached the sixth page, he spoke about his contingencies and the safe place where he intended to store supplies in case the worst happened. He also talked about a plan to run and draw attention away from me. And for the first time I felt like someone truly cared about me.

Of course, his plan hadn't worked. They had come after me anyway.

"Does this mean all three of those shadow catchers were after me, and not hoping I would lead them to him like we thought?" I asked.

"Not necessarily. They might still think he was up to something. He said he was protecting you, but not what from or who this ally of his is. And he's not repeating your phrase through this journal. Normally when a phrase runs out, it's just repeated. But he's gone somewhere else with it, and that means we can't translate any more of it without a new clue."

I exhaled, feeling some of the earlier frustration come back. We had just enough information to be worried.

Ben looked thoughtful as he studied the last page he'd

translated. "I think I know what he's referring to when he talks about stashing supplies and the first copy of the journal. He had a boat."

"Yes," I replied, reacting to the excitement in Ben's voice. "He told me he kept a boat north of LA's main beaches. It was out of the way but still close enough that he could sail down. And something about lobster pots."

"Lobster pots?"

"Yeah. Now and then, he brought back lobsters he'd caught, and we ate them for dinner. He knew how to make them taste so good."

Ben chuckled, and it quickly turned into a full belly laugh.

"What's so funny?" I asked.

"He really did intend for you and me to work together. You have no idea..." Ben's voice trailed off and a hint of sadness appeared in the lines around his eyes.

"Does this mean we know where to find him?" I asked.

"It means I know where to look next."

"You're not going without me. Anthony was my friend, and you need me to help find him."

"It's dangerous, Scarlet." Ben shifted so he could look me in the eye. "There are bound to be more shadow catchers, and while I hope to find Anthony and rescue him, I can't easily keep you safe and do that."

"Before you say another word, I won't take no for an answer. Unless I'm a prisoner here and the guards will keep me from leaving, I am coming with you. I've faced three shadow catchers before and survived. I *have* to come with you. Besides, there might be more in this journal that I can translate along the way."

Ben set his jaw as if he were going to argue with me. I held his gaze, wanting him to understand how determined I was. This was important to me. I would tear down a tower if it stood between me and helping a friend, and to frell with the consequences.

"You are a red dragon. Fierce, with a hot head, but also loyal and courageous. If you can channel your fire, you will become great."

"Awesome, but I'll settle for channeling it into finding Anthony for now."

He let out another short laugh.

"Okay. But I need you to understand that if I give you an instruction out there, I'm doing it to save your life or mine, or both. I won't always have time to explain."

"Got it. Obey panicked orders without question and then be a pain in the butt about it when we're safe. I can do that."

"I bet you can." Ben rolled his eyes as he got up and grabbed his jacket off the back of the chair.

I grabbed my bag and shoved the journal and our translated notes inside. I hesitated over the book that had helped us and looked at Ben.

"Take it. I'll clear it with Miss This-Is-My-Domain-And-Nothing-Happens-Here-Without-My Say-So downstairs."

I grinned at Ben's description of her, wondering if I was the only person who had disagreed with her over the years. It hadn't taken long to get on her bad side. Admittedly, my entrance had a style she hadn't appreciated.

I followed Ben back down to the main floor. No sooner had we reached the bottom of the stairs than she appeared.

"Done?" she asked.

"Yes, and I need to take one of the books with me. I have a feeling Anthony will have left us a trail, and I am going to need to reference some source material as we hunt for him."

The librarian frowned and eyed him up and down.

"You don't have a pocket big enough for any of my books, Ben. Therefore, I can only assume this reckless companion of yours has the book you've no doubt already taken."

Ben nodded slowly, almost as if he were expecting this to be a trap and he didn't know the correct reply.

"If anything happens to the book you've entrusted to your young ward, I will hold you personally responsible for replacing it. Is that clear?"

"Entirely, Margaret. You're the guardian of this library because you have the steel and determination to ensure it is preserved and treated with reverence and care."

This seemed to soften her a little, her cheeks coloring.

"Just see you bring it back as unblemished as you took it."

"Always."

Ben flicked me a wink as she turned on her heel and strode back to a small desk in the corner. We went to the outer door.

"How comfortable do you feel with flying?" he asked.

"So far, I've flown twice here, and both times, other dragons have tried to force me out of the air," I replied, already wishing I wasn't in the dragon city but relieved at being able to go somewhere else. Even with the threat of shadow catchers.

"It will get easier with time," Ben said, but his tone was a little flatter than usual. Almost as if he didn't believe it himself.

Without another word, I leaped out the door and focused on transforming. It wasn't the easiest thing to do, but I'd done it twice, and I wasn't alone. My wings emerged, and I flapped them. A moment later, Ben was near me in dragon form.

You've learned how to do that fast.

I had a lot of motivation, I thought.

Sounds like it. Young dragons can be as cruel to those who are different as I hear human teenagers are.

Yeah, that's about right.

Ben spent the next few minutes guiding me around towers toward the small section of land near the cliff side of the city where there was a small parking lot and a road connected to the cliff.

It didn't take me long to realize he was guiding me back to the car we'd traveled here in. The familiar vehicle was welcome, although I still longed for the comfort of my apartment and Anthony's. I had only felt safe in those two places.

After we landed and morphed into human form, I noticed two black dragons and the woman who had greeted us had appeared, the dragons flanking her semi-human form.

"Are you leaving again so soon, Ben?" she asked.

"If you'll give me the all-clear, Capricia."

"You know we prefer that you do so when it's dark and not a busy time of day," Capricia said, the same haughty tone she'd used the first time I'd met her.

Wondering what it was about female dragons taking their jobs so seriously in this dragon haven, I tried to look as calm as possible and trust that Ben knew what he was doing. The last thing I wanted was to engage in another argument with a stubborn woman over something someone else had decided.

"You know that's not something I'd flout lightly," Ben explained. "Anthony needs our help, and we finally have some idea where he might be. He's already been missing for several days, and we need to hurry."

"But you take an untrained illegal with you?"

"Anthony is linked to her. He trusts her. Even more than he trusts me."

Her eyes went wide before she turned her gaze on me, and I got the impression Ben had said something that carried a lot of weight. What had happened in the past that made everyone aware of Anthony and Ben being there for each other?

"All right. But you should take this." The woman reached into a pocket in her robe and pulled out a small, glowing orb.

"Set it off if you need us, and we'll send our best."

Ben took it hesitantly. "I truly hope I don't need to use it."

"As do I, but it would be wrong to lose you and your ward if Anthony truly did as you say he did."

"Come on, Scarlet," Ben said, seeming to become uncomfortable with her attention. "Let's go find him."

CHAPTER SIXTEEN

We drove in silence, the world moving around us as if we were simply sitting in the car and it was traveling underneath and to each side of us. Too many thoughts raced around my head for me to want to talk much, and I was feeling too many different emotions.

The weight on my shoulders to translate Anthony's journal, the fear he might not be alive, and the anxiety about how everyone else had been treating me in the city were making me feel both lightheaded and sick. The only consolation I had was a possible new home. As long as the bullies calmed down, of course.

I'd learned so much in a few days, but I still had so far to go. Apparently, dragons had been hiding for centuries because they were hunted by humans, but they believed humanity needed them. No one had explained why humans needed us, however.

I wondered if it was because of the shadow catchers, and if there was something about the way they hunted us that meant they weren't focusing on humans. The monsters were scary enough that I could see why they weren't the first focus in a school setting. But Ben had alluded to them working for something or someone else and being almost mindless minions. No one had made any mention of any other kind of force either.

On top of that, no one had explained what red dragons had done to be so hated either. No one knew why Anthony thought I needed protecting, except that I was a red dragon and, as everyone kept calling me, an illegal.

I had gotten some answers on that, at least. All dragon children had to be approved by a board. Apparently they almost never said no, but they made sure there weren't too many young dragons in an area at once. Also, they monitored the color lines so they either stayed pure or allowed for certain combinations.

I'd been interested in that part of the class, and it opened up even larger questions. Now wasn't the time for them, however. And I knew that meant I needed to pick and choose the most important ones.

"Everyone keeps calling me your ward," I said, not sure how else to introduce my curiosity.

"Yes. Your tablet should have beeped you to let you know it was approved."

"I don't have a tablet, if you're referring to that glowing thing that other dragons are controlling with their minds."

"That explains a few things. You should have been given one in your first class and shown how to use it."

"So that's why everyone laughed at me when I took notes on paper." I sighed.

I was getting a bit sick of being treated like a crazed

hermit. At some point, I was going to have to teach someone a lesson and earn some respect the hard way.

"I'm sorry. I know it's not easy being an outsider, and it's also not easy being a red dragon in these times. Being both... I'll make sure that the tablet is sorted. I'm sorry."

"Not your fault. Let's just find Anthony. Then I can go back to my apartment and my normal life."

"I was hoping you might want to stay in the city and keep learning," Ben replied, his voice sounding wistful.

"Yeah, 'cause I'd love to stay in a city where a lot of them want to hurt me for being red, and everyone else is laughing at me for not knowing about dragons. It's the perfect welcoming environment."

"I know it's far from ideal. I'll understand if you don't want to stay, but I won't deny I hope for a particular future."

"Like what?" I asked. He was a good person. I could humor him.

"That Anthony comes with you and stops hiding. Now you've been to the city, and everyone knows about you. I'm not sure what he could be hiding you from that could get to you if you live with us."

"Your guess is as good as mine at this point. Is that why people are talking about me being your ward?" I asked, still not sure what was going on.

"I offered to be your ward and sponsor your education and training in lieu of parents stepping forward. The system wouldn't let me do it at first because of the color difference. The elders opted to allow it in this circumstance, given the odds of a color match are extremely low. I'm now entirely responsible for you and your antics until you graduate. If you go back to living in LA and break the rules, I will be punished alongside you."

"Oh." My voice came out smaller and quieter than I had originally intended. That wasn't what I'd expected him to say. "Thank you."

"Don't mention it. I'm certain it's what Anthony would have done if things were reversed."

"Then let's hope we find him. He can take your place, and you won't have to worry about the trouble I cause."

That earned me another small laugh and lightened the mood. We were looking for our missing friend and facing an unknown level of danger, but I felt more positive. I wasn't alone, and Ben cared enough to make sure I never would be, even if he had done it on Anthony's behalf.

We talked about the history of dragons as we drove the rest of the way, Ben explaining that dragons protected against certain dangers, but those weren't a good topic while we were driving into danger. He also explained that dragons had been almost hunted to extinction. Hiding from humanity had been necessary.

It struck me that it must be hard to hide from and be hurt by the very people you were trying to protect. I recalled the times I had been a bit of a brat to Anthony, especially at first. Now that I had more of an idea of what he'd been doing for me, I wondered if he'd ever despaired at my treatment of him.

As we drove the final section of the road to a small town north of LA, I looked through the journal, trying to figure out what the keywords for the next set of pages might be. The first phrase had come to me as I'd thought about Anthony and what we did together and how he treated me, so I tried the same trick again. I told Ben about our habits and the things we liked to do.

"I'm not surprised he liked to play board games with you. You've got a bright mind, and he liked a challenge. They also stop him from overthinking." Ben pulled the car into a tiny parking lot. There was a row of beach huts nearby.

I blinked a few times in the fading sunlight, worried that it was getting late and we didn't know where to begin looking for him.

It wasn't ideal, but nothing in the last few days had been. I was just grateful we had a lead and we didn't have any shadow catchers after us.

Both of us got out of the car and moved toward the water.

"Time to look for signs of Anthony being here. Given how little we have to go on, but how he seems to be making a trail for us to follow, there ought to be some kind of clue somewhere around here."

I wasn't going to argue. Ben knew more about Anthony by far. We were the right team for this hunt and I was in good hands looking for my friend alongside him.

We started by going south along the waterfront, where the beach huts were, and in the direction of LA. Wherever Anthony kept his boat, it wasn't far from the city.

The setting sun bathed the fronts of the huts in stunning colors. We marveled at them for a moment before Ben pointed at one of the painted huts further down. He hurried up to it and gestured at the roof.

"That symbol. It's in the dragon language. It means peace," Ben said, looking more than a little excited.

For a moment, I didn't move or respond. Was it going to be this easy?

There was no way to be sure, but Ben didn't let me ponder for long. He felt around the edge of the door for a key. I worked my way down to the gap between the huts on one side. It was narrow, and I had to squeeze, but I made it to the back and spotted a small box on the back of the hut. It looked like a small key safe.

"Four numbers, and I can get us access," I called.

"Genius. Try thirteen forty-two," Ben called back.

I tapped in the numbers, and it opened immediately, the front coming off in one hand, and the key dropping down into the other. I let out a delighted laugh.

"How did you know?" I asked as I started the wriggle to get back to the front of the hut.

"That was his lucky number plus the meaning of life, the universe, and everything."

Ben must have known him so well. For a moment I felt a stab of pain in my chest, a little jealous he'd known something about Anthony I hadn't. I tried not to let it get to me, however.

"That was a clever idea. A gap only you could have fitted through and a combination only I could have known." Ben took the key as I got to the end of the hut and held it out.

His words made me feel better. This whole mission did seem designed to get the two of us working together. I was as important as Ben was. Neither of us could complete it without the other.

Ben soon had the door open, and the dying light revealed the interior of an orderly beach hut. The walls were lined with shelves and cupboards, and a small table stood with two folding chairs leaning against one side. A kitchenette was on the opposite side. It had everything a person would need to camp out except a bed.

"Thank the gates. The shadow catchers haven't found it yet." Ben walked inside and went to the cupboards.

There was food in them, but it was only partially stocked, and disturbed dust showed that someone had been here and taken some of the supplies recently.

Ben and I pulled everything from each cupboard and checked for hidden objects or compartments. I removed several cans of soup and vegetables, impressed by the variety.

While we searched for anything out of the ordinary, the light faded until we could no longer see.

"How about you shed a bit more light?" Ben asked. He pulled the door shut behind us and almost blocked out what was left of the fading sunlight and prevent anyone from seeing inside.

Confused by the question, I didn't know how to respond.

"You do know that you can control light and dark, right?" he asked. "You can make any area brighter, centered on a single point. And with practice, multiple sources are possible. Using yourself as the source is easiest."

I nodded as if I'd known this all along, but the little I'd known was that I could make it dark when I really wanted to hide. And I hadn't attempted it when I wasn't in serious need of the end result.

Closing my eyes, I remembered how it had felt to make things dark but thought about making the area brighter instead. Now and then I opened my eyes but I was still standing in the dark. Although I couldn't be sure, I felt Ben staring at me.

"You haven't attempted this before, have you?" he asked.

"I think we both know the answer to that question. If you want to have any chance of making this work and seeing what's in here without a flashlight, you need to let me try until I figure it out."

"Oh, I have flashlights. It's just better if you do it."

I opened my mouth to tell him it was stupid to make me try to light up the room when we had perfectly good alternatives as well as how unfair that was on me, and how I didn't appreciate the pressure, when I started to glow. As the room got brighter, I saw the grin on his face.

"Perfect. I wondered if making you angry would help. Typical red dragon. Pressure or anger does it every time."

Not sure if I should thank him or smack him, I focused on the task at hand. We needed to find anything that might lead us to Anthony's boat or, better, to him.

We searched until I was getting fed up with rummaging through cupboards. There was plenty of food, spare parts, a first aid kit, and a pile of books we'd flipped through.

Not sure what else to do, I moved to the little kitchenette and pulled open the cupboard under the burners. I wasn't sure what I'd find. Maybe a trash can or something. Instead, I found a small safe bolted to the floor.

My surprised squeak let Ben know I'd discovered something.

"Well, that was obvious. I feel foolish," Ben said as we crouched to get a better look at it.

"I don't suppose it will be the same combination as the

key safe outside?" I asked, pretty sure I knew the answer already. It wouldn't be. These things were never that easy.

Ben laughed, confirming my suspicion. We needed different numbers.

"Okay, this has to be something we'd work out. Something we'd know between us."

The only thing I could think of was the day Anthony had met me and this had all begun. It was the only other set of numbers that wouldn't be obvious to anyone else.

I reached out and turned the dial, putting the numbers in, not entirely expecting it to work. To my surprise, it did, and the safe swung open. Inside were keys and a folded map.

With shaking hands, I pulled everything out and handed the keys to Ben, not trusting myself with them. They had a large string ball attached to them, something that looked like it would float if dropped in the water.

Ben took them as I unfolded the map.

"It's a chart with markings that someone added to it," I said, focusing the light I was producing where we needed it.

"Perfect. And there's a boat name and number in the common dragon language at the top of the map. Look." Ben pointed at something scrawled up there. Excited, I couldn't stop my hands from shaking. We were doing it. We were finding the trail Anthony had left for us.

We stood, and I dimmed the light a little again. I then tucked the map into my bag, along with the journal and notes we already had, and gave Ben a nod. It was time to locate Anthony's boat and see what we could find out at sea. It was our next clue.

CHAPTER SEVENTEEN

No sooner had we locked the beach hut again, with everything replaced but a packet of cookies Ben had decided would make a good snack, when a noise startled us. A slithering, almost hissing noise.

A chill ran up my spine. It wasn't a noise I'd heard a lot, but it was a noise I was familiar with.

Shadow catchers.

And I could feel them. Two of them, creeping down the path we'd taken a short while earlier. They were getting closer with every moment.

I held up two fingers and pointed in their direction, not daring to speak after my previous encounters with them. Ben pointed the other way, and we turned to leave.

It was hard to be entirely silent, but we did our best, moving across the ground as quickly as we could manage in the sand. I also kept half my mind focused on the shadow catchers.

We put some distance between us when they stopped at the beach house. And it wasn't long before a crunching sound filled the night air. I stopped and looked back, but Ben took my hand and shook his head.

"There's nothing we can do to save it," he whispered so quietly that I could barely hear him.

I knew he was right, but I wanted to go back and rescue some of the stuff in there. I knew the books would have meant something to Anthony. Thankfully, the library tome we'd brought with us was safe in my bag. I hoped it would remain that way if we were going to be on the run from shadow catchers again.

My brain buzzed with questions for Ben. Wondering how we could survive the night, I hoped he knew how to get away from the creatures that seemed able to track us. Because we had to find Anthony, and I didn't want to give up. There was no way I would stop looking for my mentor this time.

Not again.

I didn't dare speak my thoughts, too aware of the danger behind us and how easily the monsters detected noise. It was just too high a risk, especially after I had promised not to be a pain in the butt until we were safe.

As we hurried south, it didn't take me long to realize that Ben was trying to find Anthony's boat as we ran. Given that the shadow catchers appeared to literally feed off water for energy, the idea of risking our lives on a boat filled me with dread.

I had just opened my mouth to protest this very thing when Ben stopped at a small harbor and the main jetty where the boat was most likely to be moored.

Ben turned to me and noticed. He put his hand to his mouth, and motioned for me to be quiet. Although I wanted to growl my frustration, the question a valid one given the situation, I didn't do that either. My fear of being noticed by the shadow catchers was greater than my lack of trust in Ben right now.

He beckoned for me to follow him, but we didn't get far before he motioned for me to crouch. I did so along with him, both of us hidden by the boats on either side

Looking around us, Ben seemed to hesitate. I wanted to ask why, but again I waited. After a brief pause, he looked back at me again and seemed to lean in for a hug.

Instead of hugging me, he whispered, "I need you to light the sides of the boats just enough to see their names."

I could have hit myself for not noticing the problem and doing something about it sooner.

As he pulled back, I concentrated on making only my hand glow like a flashlight, small and dim enough that I could hide with the rest of my body.

It took me a few seconds to get it to work, and I wasn't sure I had succeeded, but slowly, I brightened it until I could just about see the edge of the boat and was able to make out the name.

This wasn't the boat we were looking for, so we hurried to the next, then the next, crouching so the boats shielded us from both sides until we found the right one.

As we progressed down the dock, I felt the shadow catchers getting closer and closer, and it made me more nervous. What if this was all in vain and we ended up trapped?

The shadow creatures were at the entrance to the dock when we found the right boat. It was a small yacht but it looked like it had a motor as well as sails, and it was at the end of the dock, so we wouldn't have a problem reaching the open sea.

Without hesitation, Ben ushered me up onto the deck and ran to undo the nearest mooring rope. I got on and took the rope, then helped him on. He brought the second rope with him. Once again, I used my hand as a light so we could put the key in the ignition.

At first Ben didn't turn it but looked around.

"We need to go," I whispered, daring to speak for the first time.

"They're going to hear it the second I turn this on," he replied equally quietly.

"Then we shouldn't hang around after you do."

Our eyes met, barely able to see each other in the dark. This wasn't going to be easy, but it was all we had and I didn't want to give up now.

Ben looked at the key again, hesitating, but then turned it and brought the engine to life. He quickly put it into drive and then stared at the wheel as if he wasn't sure what to do next.

Rolling my eyes, I reached out and pushed the throttle lever forward, giving the boat some momentum. It took a second to show signs of working, but then the boat started moving—but the engine made even more noise. The shadow catchers picked up on it even from so far away, and I felt them come closer in my mind, filling me with dread.

I exhaled, trying to will the boat to go faster, but we needed to make sure we didn't hit anything, and we'd also have to navigate the harbor exit.

"Hurry," I said. "They're coming up fast."

"It's okay. They can't follow us out here. Probably. That's one of the reasons Anthony has a boat."

"They can't?" I replied, neither of us trying to be quiet now that the engine noise had given us away.

"No. They can absorb water, but they can't swim very easily. If they're in the water too long, they explode."

I blinked a few times, my whole body relaxing when I realized we were safe, but it was soon replaced by anger.

"Why didn't you tell me?" The anger came out in my words as I bunched my fists.

"Easy, Red. I didn't have a good opportunity."

"Don't call me 'Red.' It's 'Scarlet.'" I let out a growl and flicked the boat's lights on so we could see where we were going.

"Thank you." Ben gave me a small salute as if I were the captain, and did his best to navigate the boat until we were out on open water. I pulled out the map Anthony had left us and looked at the panel of instruments we had to work with to give us an idea of where we needed to go and how to get to the first marked point. We would have to use the GPS to find the coordinates.

It took a while to figure out how to get the boat going in the right direction and what all the dials meant, but we had a compass, a speedometer, instruments that measured wind direction and speed, a depth gauge, and a GPS. The latter was the most useful and we were soon heading for the area we wanted.

I tried not to think about where Anthony was if he hadn't chosen to take his boat. I wanted him to be safe, but he was leading us down a trail the shadow catchers were also on. Would they find him before we did?

Although Ben appeared calm, his knuckles were white as he gripped the wheel. This was getting to him too.

"You care about Anthony a lot, don't you?" I asked.

Ben nodded, and I thought that was the end of our conversation, but he tilted his head to the side a moment later.

"Anthony is the sort of dragon who could look at you and see right through everything to the core of you. But instead of feeling naked, it makes you feel seen. Like you're safe while that vulnerable."

There was no arguing with that assessment of Anthony. He had done similar with me.

"He cares about you too, then?" I asked.

"Yes. We were...together for many years, and I never felt more loved or alive. I didn't understand why he had to leave Detaris, but he said he would put me in danger by telling me."

"I'm sorry," was all I said, not sure what else to say.

Although I'd suspected they'd had more than a friendship between them, it was confirmation and I didn't want to push him to share something that was so personal and clearly still hurting him.

"I understand now. He was protecting you, and even if I still don't know why, it's clear that you also mean a lot to him, and he believed in his reasons. When we find him, I will tell him the same thing, and we'll figure out what needs to happen next together."

I nodded and, without really thinking about it, I reached out my hand and placed it over Ben's.

"Together." I looked him in the eye.

In response, he twisted his hand to squeeze my fingers, then echoed the word back at me.

We stayed like that for a while, neither of us wanting to let go of the other, both hunting for the same person, knowing he meant the world to both of us in different ways.

Finally, we reached the first of the buoys that marked the lobster pots Anthony regularly checked. It was strange to think of this being something Anthony had done for pleasure as well as a way to leave a trail. When it took us several minutes to get the boat anchored so we could haul up the first pot, I decided this wasn't a fun pastime.

It wasn't the easiest thing to pull up, and the chain was slimy with gunk. There was even the odd sea creature that came up with it, flopping onto the deck or being knocked back by our hands. It was disgusting, especially in the dark. Finally, we brought the lobster pot aboard, though we got wet in the process. Although there was a lobster inside and it tried to pinch us through the pot, it wasn't what we were looking for.

"Chuck it back?" Ben asked.

"Doesn't that kill them or something? The air gets trapped in their shells?"

"I think that's crabs, and a myth."

"Oh. Then, up to you. We haven't had dinner yet." I looked at my filthy hands and the gross lobster pot. I didn't want to eat the crustacean, but I couldn't deny that I was hungry.

Ben opted to keep it, disconnecting the cage from the line and moving it to one side of the deck.

I hauled the anchor back up, ready to get to the next

one and hoping that Anthony didn't make us pull up too many of these things before we found what we wanted.

Three lobster pots later, I was fed up. My lower half was soaked, my hands were so cold they hurt, and they were caked in filth. Ben hadn't fared any better, but he was managing not to be snappy.

"We'll get one more," he said as he tucked our third lobster pot against the side of the boat. We'd put the empty cage back but kept the rest, and I didn't think the creatures appreciated the process any more than we did.

I shivered as we got back to the helm to go to the next one, so cold now that I couldn't hold up under the cool breeze blowing across the water.

"Come closer," Ben said, putting out an arm as if to pull me into a hug.

I hesitated, as that would double up the smell of rancid seawater and he was also soaking and filthy.

"You're just as dirty and wet. Come on. I can make us both warmer, and it will keep you from getting sick."

That was all the persuasion I needed, although I wasn't sure he could offer me much warmth to make it entirely worth it. I didn't have anything to lose, however. Moving in closer, I let him put his arm around me and tuck me against him.

As soon as I could feel some contact between the two of us, he seemed to heat up, becoming far hotter than a normal human. It was like being snuggled up to a body-length hot-water bottle.

"Is this your dragon power?" I asked, surprised but grateful.

"Yes. Heat and cold. I can freeze things too, but we don't need that right now."

I chuckled and shook my head as we reached the next location. Having had practice, we worked as a team to get the boat into place and get the anchor down.

This time as I went to pull up the lobster pot, I did so with renewed energy. Ben's warmth had helped me focus. We worked together, soon getting the chain up. Inside the trap on the end of this one, there was a large metal box with solid walls and a sealed door.

For a few seconds, all we could both do was stare at it, the box on the boat with us. With shaking hands, Ben undid the chain and let the pot fall back into the sea, leaving us with the box it had brought up.

"We should open it before we get to shore, just in case," I said when it looked like he was going to head toward the coast.

I got no argument from him as we both sat in front of the strange door on the box and tried to work out how to open it. It took us a moment, but we figured it out and it sprang open, revealing a dry interior. The contents were stowed in a vacuum bag that had most of the air squashed out of it.

I reached for the bag but pulled back. I had previously been enthusiastic about opening it, but now there was a part of me that was nervous. Would we be led on somewhere else, or was this finally going to lead us to Anthony? And what was the point of all of this?

There was only one way to find out, yet neither of us could bring ourselves to open the bag.

CHAPTER EIGHTEEN

We were almost back to our starting point when Ben pulled the helm over and brought the ship around to head north up the coast instead of back into the harbor.

I opened my mouth to question it a fraction of a second before I sensed three of the shadow catchers on the shore nearby. Not wanting to draw their attention, I kept silent and held up three fingers and pointed in their direction in case Ben hadn't felt them like I did.

He nodded to acknowledge that he'd seen my motions and then took the boat a little further out from shore. I tried not to worry as we moved, sensing the frightening creatures that were pursuing us. Thankfully, they seemed to get left behind, unaware that we were traveling past them out at sea.

When I hadn't been able to feel them for several minutes, I relaxed. They were scarier than any monster I'd imagined as a child, and I didn't want to encounter another one as long as I lived.

"Where are we heading?" I asked a short while later, when we were still traveling up the coast.

"I want to get north of the car so we can circle back to it. Then I think we need to find some food. Maybe trade these lobsters for food that's been cooked."

My stomach rumbled almost as soon as Ben finished speaking, which made him chuckle. We agreed on the food part of the plan, although, having seen the grimy lobsters in their pots, I was less excited about eating them for dinner anymore. Whenever I'd eaten them with Anthony, they had already been cleaned, if not cooked, by the time I got to his house.

This was a part of the process I hadn't seen. It appeared as if I was going to learn something at every stage of this strange hunt. Even if it wasn't something I was expecting.

By the time Ben stopped the boat's engine, we were much further north, and I was exhausted. But we were also still a long way out to sea. As he moved to the anchor, I opened my mouth to voice my concern about how we were going to get to shore.

He preempted me.

"There's a lifeboat thing that blows itself up." He pointed to a white box.

I could have hit myself for not noticing it, but it had been a difficult night, and we hadn't focused on anything but the lobster pots and the dry box we'd found.

We'd fished the plastic bag from it but hadn't opened it yet, agreeing it was best kept safely sealed until we had it ashore, in the car, and we had food. We could look at it while we ate.

Very eager to get as far from the shadow catchers as

possible, I wasn't going to argue. Instead, I helped Ben to get the anchor down one last time and gather everything we wanted to take with us. Only then did we dare tackle the life raft.

Picture-based instructions were printed on the side of the container, but they weren't particularly useful when we were trying not to draw attention to ourselves. I barely dared to make my hand glow.

Eventually, we figured it out and had a blowup raft with sides and a paddle sitting in the water beside the yacht. It didn't look like it had ever been used, but we were about to put the contraption to the test.

"You get in, and I'll pass you everything." Ben offered a hand to help me board the smaller craft.

I didn't like the idea of being the first to get inside, but I didn't want to have to pick up the lobster pots and figure out a way to hand them over either. At least I would only have to accept them and then lower them to sit around my feet.

The raft wasn't as firm as I expected, and it bent when I put my foot down. Already committed, I put the other foot in and leaned toward the other edge.

Ben let go of me, but before I could get settled and try to take the first item from him, a wave came past and the raft lurched. I wobbled and fell into the water.

I gasped, inhaling some water as the icy cold liquid hit my skin. Then I was underneath, flailing and trying to find the surface. Fear tore through me, adding to the pain of the freezing water and the burning in my lungs as my body tried to cough and splutter.

Having just enough sense not to try to breathe, I began

to calm down, doing everything I could to work out which way was up, but there was no light to guide me. I made myself glow a little, hoping Ben would find me or the light I gave off would show where the bottom was. We were close to shore, and the bottom wouldn't be too far below us. I hoped.

After a few agonizing seconds that made my chest ache even more and my body fight to breathe, a darker object came toward me.

Ben.

He grabbed me and tucked an arm around my waist. At first, even more fear coursed through me. What if we both drowned? Then who would find Anthony?

Forcing myself to calm, I managed to gather myself to help Ben. I kicked my legs and pulled us in the same direction with my arms. My lungs felt as if they were on fire, and it took all my self-control not to cough or inhale before we broke the surface.

The cool night air felt wonderful on my face, but I started coughing and spluttering as Ben kept me afloat.

"Not too loud, Scarlet," he said, barely above a whisper but loud enough that I could hear him over the noise I was making.

I fought the desire to cough when I remembered the shadow catchers out there.

As soon as Ben was sure I was all right, he let go of me. I followed him as he swam toward the larger boat. We were a little way off it, but it wouldn't take long to get back. And the raft was floating nearby, although it was now upside-down and bobbing in the waves.

I didn't want to get back into the unstable craft, but we

had little choice. With all the noise I'd made on the water, there was a chance we'd been heard. I didn't want to hang around.

Shivering and drenched, I helped Ben flip the inflatable over. He held it in place while I climbed down the ladder of the yacht and got into the raft again. This time, I kept my body lower and flopped into it, making a squelching noise in my waterlogged clothes. I wanted to cry. I could swim, and water didn't bother me, but there had been so many difficult days in a row that I couldn't take it anymore.

Instead of letting my emotions out, I let Ben hand me everything we were taking with us, item by item. Despite wanting to hurry, we transferred everything carefully. The whole time I knelt, making sure I didn't over balance.

I didn't enjoy taking the slimy lobster pots off him and I narrowly missed being pinched a couple of times. Eventually they were stowed on the other side of the raft. The sealed bag was next.

Finally, Ben handed me my pack, which I was glad I hadn't brought with me the first time I'd tried to get into the raft. The library book, the journal, and the things we'd translated were in it, and it wasn't waterproof. Not sure what else to do with it, I stowed it carefully on top of the sealed bag, keeping it off the wet raft bottom and making it as safe as I could under the circumstances.

With everything on the raft, Ben tried to join me. I moved back as he leaned slowly over, grateful that the weight of the lobster pots counterbalanced everything.

We wobbled a bit, but eventually, he was in.

After picking up a paddle each, we slowly rowed to shore. At first, it felt like we weren't making any progress, the waves bobbing us about more and more, but every time I looked back, the yacht was further away. Finally, it was lost in the dark.

I paddled faster, wanting to be on shore and dry. The breeze was freezing, and the weight of the water in my clothes made my limbs tired. My fingers were numb, and I was only maintaining a grip on the paddle because my hands were locked in place.

We got closer and closer to the section of shore where the waves were breaking. They were high enough that they could flip us if we weren't careful, but we had momentum now, and I didn't think we could have stopped ourselves from hitting the shore if we'd wanted to.

Ben realized the same danger and stopped paddling, letting us glide, then paddling furiously to catch a promising wave.

I joined him, trusting his judgment, and we crested a wave and rode it to shore. It carried us up the beach until the weight of our raft made us catch on the bottom. When the water receded, Ben stuck his paddle down and held us firm.

Not wanting to be on the raft a second longer, I got out and grabbed one side. My feet were only in a few inches of water, but it was very cold.

As soon as Ben was out, he grabbed a section of the raft as well, and we pulled it up the beach. It slid across the wet sand easily, although it made a lot of noise, but not as much as on drier sand, which slowed our advance.

Eventually, we couldn't move it any further.

"We need to get these to the car. Can you carry a couple of lobster pots?" Ben whispered.

I considered asking if the lobsters were worth it, but it didn't feel right to waste them. And we did need to eat something.

After fetching my bag and slinging it over my shoulder, I let Ben hand me a couple of the pots and held them out far enough that the creatures inside couldn't do more than snap their large claws in my direction. They didn't seem to appreciate being carried, and I almost dropped one as the lobster lurched and unbalanced the pot.

With a little luck, I managed to keep hold of it. I took a moment to make sure my grip was firm, then followed Ben again. We quietly walked along the beachfront and hoped we could get out of the area before the shadow catchers found us.

It wasn't an easy task.

As the minutes ticked by, the ache in my arms deepened from holding the lobster pots up and out of the way. It was agonizing by the time Ben spotted the parking lot. A few lamps were still on, and the car was visible ahead of us.

I couldn't feel any shadow catchers nearby and there didn't seem to be any we could see or hear. It was a relief after the evening we'd had. We were both still wet, but movement kept me from shivering. I didn't doubt that Ben had the same problem.

When I reached Ben's car, I put the lobster pots down near the trunk and paused. I didn't want to get the seats wet, but we didn't have any towels.

"It's okay. Get inside. We've got to get warm," Ben said as he popped the trunk and motioned for me to get into the passenger seat.

I still hesitated, worried about the car's interior. It was

salt water. However, I wouldn't be surprised if some dragon magic superpower could clean it up. Maybe even make it as if nothing had happened at all. Either way, I was glad I didn't have to stand out in the cold any longer or worry about lobster pots, and I hurried to get inside.

Ben gave me the waterproof bag and loaded the lobster pots, and a moment later, he was in the car and pulling out of the parking lot. Only when the beach was in the rearview mirror and I still couldn't feel any shadow catchers could I recover.

The tension left me bit by bit, muscles relaxing through my body until I was finally at ease. Afterward, I took stock of our surroundings. Instead of going to Detaris, Ben headed toward LA, but he pulled into the parking lot of an all-night diner before we reached the outskirts.

I wanted to ask if he had any money as I had none of my own, but it was so late I wasn't sure a place like this was even serving food.

"Come on," he said. "They know our kind here. We'll be able to get fed and trade these lobsters for something really good. Do you like steak?"

I nodded, loving the plan. Ben had more of a handle on this mission than I'd thought.

CHAPTER NINETEEN

Stuffed with steak and potatoes, I leaned back in a booth at the rear of the diner. I was dry, Ben having used his powers to dry my clothes; I had locked myself into a toilet cubicle and handed each piece over the top. He'd dried his clothes in the same manner.

On the table in front of us was the bag from the safe, now empty, and a copy of Anthony's journal. Around it were all sorts of other things. Another map, hand-drawn, with no locations marked on it. It meant nothing to either of us.

We also found some notes. Many of these were handwritten and seemed unimportant, but others were useful, like a method of stunning a shadow catcher. It required a bright light to flash suddenly, something I felt I was more than qualified to do.

On top of that, there were a couple of blank pieces of paper, randomly in with everything else. I had no idea what they were for.

"Here you go," the chef said as she headed to our table.

She had a parcel wrapped in brown paper and what looked like food inside. "Sandwiches, cake, and I cooked up one of those lobsters to go, in garlic. It will need eating before too long unless you've got a way of keeping it cold."

"Thank you, Betty. You've done wonders." Ben smiled at her like she was the only person in the world, and she flushed. I was almost entirely ignored as she told him to travel safely and went back to the kitchen.

"Okay, back to the car. We shouldn't discuss this in a public setting." Ben got up, dropped a twenty on the table despite the food we'd traded, and headed for the door.

After shoving the papers back into the bag, along with the extra journal, I followed him. By the time I reached the car, the heater was on. I expected to sit there and talk, but he put the car into drive and pulled out of the parking lot. He drove north, back into the countryside.

As soon as we came to a country lane that appeared to drive into some woods, Ben turned up the track and slowed to bump along for a few hundred meters before he pulled to one side and stopped.

"Let's figure out where Anthony went next." Ben reached for the pack, and I let him pull everything out.

I was impatient to figure out what came next too, but I couldn't make heads or tails of our new find after half an hour of staring at it. This wasn't like finding a boat name, ignition keys, and a marked-up map to work with. This was something else entirely. And I wondered if we needed to translate more of the journal.

If we did, I had no idea what the phrase for the next section was. I couldn't think of anything else he used to say to me, and I was tired of these games. I just wanted my mentor back.

Ben broke the silence. "I never thought of Anthony as the sort of person who wasted anything or put something where it didn't belong."

"No. He was always precise," I replied, wondering where he was going with this.

He held up the blank pieces of paper.

"What if these aren't as blank as they look?"

I frowned, not entirely sure what he could mean, but curious enough to want to find out. Possibly, Anthony would have thought to put something on them.

I held one up and lit up my hand again, trying to see it better. At first, it looked the same as the rest of the paper, but when I brought my hand closer and tilted the paper to the side, I detected something under the surface. It was like it wanted to be seen but somehow wasn't.

"I think there *is* something here, but it's hidden," I said.

"Show me." Ben leaned in as well.

It took several attempts, but I eventually managed to show him what I was seeing and he nodded.

"Keep your hand there and make the light just a little bit brighter," he said as he brought his hand up beside mine, both of us with our palms facing the page.

Heat emanated from his hand toward the page, and understanding dawned on me. Everything else on this hunt had required both of us. It made sense that there would be an element that required both our dragon powers too.

The combined heat and light made a few words appear on the page, a sentence about being on the water.

"What're the odds that this is what we need for the next

set of pages?" Ben asked. His eyes reflected the light as he looked at me.

I grinned. This was exactly what we needed.

As Ben reached for more paper and continued translating, I let go of the tension I'd been carrying. It had bothered me that I couldn't think of another phrase to try. Knowing I wasn't supposed to do it alone made me feel better.

I helped Ben translate eight more pages in the next hour. When we used our combined light and heat on the second blank sheet, we found it. This one was a section of map adjacent to the one we already had. It showed us a cabin and several caches.

It appeared that Anthony had built a shadow catcher hunting ground, which gave me hope that we would find him alive. He'd planned to have to hold out against them.

"How do you kill a shadow catcher?" I asked.

"You can't."

"Everything can be killed. You've just got to figure out how."

Ben looked at me as if he was going to argue but clarified his statement instead.

"They get their power from something far greater. They can be...temporarily dissipated, but because the source doesn't die, neither do they in the long term."

I got the feeling there was more to this tale and wondered if it was common dragon knowledge. Thankfully, Ben realized he needed to explain more, and he pulled out the sandwiches and lobster for us to munch while he told me the story. It was only a couple of hours since we'd left the diner, but I found I could eat a little again.

"A long time ago, dragons warred with an evil creature over Earth, the creature responsible for the shadow catchers. Humanity hid from us both. Eventually, a powerful line of red dragons figured out how to channel their energy and that of all the dragons into containing this evil."

"Ah. And this is linked to why everyone is weird about red dragons?"

"It is. But it's another story on its own. Most importantly, the evil creature is contained, and it was the red dragons who joined us together and channeled our power to trap it and make it secure. We're tied to the gate that holds it prisoner, and the dragons are still tied into that power with our magic."

"Can any red dragon do it?" I asked.

"No, and that pisses off a lot of red dragons—and everyone else."

"Fun. That also explains why dragons had to hide when humans were trying to slaughter you."

"Us? You're a dragon too. I know that's hard to get used to. But yes—dragons hid so there would be enough to protect the world."

"Sacrificial of everyone," I replied.

"Self-preservation, more like. But the point is if there are this many shadow catchers after Anthony, he was up to something that the evil creature didn't like. If I know Anthony, it had something to do with channeling the energy of the dragons. Because the line of red dragons was broken."

"Is that why he was protecting me?"

"Yeah. Sorry, kiddo, but I don't think you're the next big red dragon. The head red dragon died a while ago and left no heirs, and you're not the right age, even if he snuck off to make one."

I nodded, but something Anthony had once said echoed in the back of my mind. He'd told me I was destined for greatness, and it didn't matter who my parents were as much as my intent and my commitment. That the world told us we were one thing, and some people believed it. But that I was different. I was one of those rare few who truly got to decide for themselves, and all I had to do was choose a great path.

We both looked at each other, and I knew Ben was considering the same question I was. If Anthony wasn't protecting me because of who I was, then why was he? We were missing something.

Now wasn't the time to ask it, however. We needed to find Anthony so he could explain it himself. Or figure out more of his journal to see if that told us.

Either way, it was time to look at what we'd translated.

At first, it seemed to be nothing more than an account of him getting settled, earning my trust, and fixing more of the broken things in my apartment. He confessed to breaking something on one visit so that he had to come back again the following day and make me like him even more.

I wanted to be angry at his duplicity, but I found I couldn't be. He had been there for me, and his journal entries spoke of me with respect and admiration and his desire to not see me so alone all the time.

Ben read the words with care, pausing a couple of times before getting to the next section. The final part spoke of the woods he had chosen for a cabin and indicated that he'd had help from someone to build it, though this someone remained nameless. It gave enough detail about the woods that we laughed. We were on the road he had described. Even in the dark, it matched Anthony's description and that meant all we had to do was turn the car back on and keep going.

"Ready to go find the stubborn dragon?" Ben asked, but he needn't have bothered as I tucked one of the journals into the waterproof bag, along with the new notes, and put the older stuff back in my pack.

I didn't know if anyone or anything was following us or if we had done something to attract attention, but I knew Anthony was being very careful about who knew what, and that made me want to do the same. On top of that, Ben hadn't wanted the other dragons to know that a journal existed. What I was learning wasn't something the dragon world was united on.

However, that brought up more questions. Something in the dragon world wasn't right, and after I found Anthony, I intended to get to the bottom of that. I was linked to more than I had realized. And Anthony was trying to tell me something. Something he possibly didn't want even Ben to understand.

CHAPTER TWENTY

We bumped along the road for several miles, going ever deeper into the woods. I had to hold onto the oh-shit handle here and there as things got lumpy. I thought we were going to bottom out, but the car was built like a tank and we just kept going.

After a few miles the road ended in front of a large tree that looked like it had seen more than a few storms and barely survived the last one. I grinned at Ben as I got out of the car, pleased to note the tree was on the map in the notes. It gave us a direction to continue on foot, and I believed we were on the right track.

This whole hunt for Anthony had made me wonder what was going on in my life, but it had also gotten me out of LA. I now realized there was more to life than working, sleeping, eating, and playing games. Bigger things were going on in the world, and I wouldn't be a part of them unless I involved myself.

Not wanting to walk into tree trunks, I made my hand

glow just enough to let us move silently and efficiently through the trees.

Ben held the map and directed us, giving me the opportunity to look around. I couldn't remember the last time I'd been in a forest, and I'd never been in one at night. It was odd and more than a little scary. Every noise made me think of the shadow catchers, and every looming bush made catch my breath.

"I thought you could sense when the shadow catchers were close," Ben whispered when I jumped for the fifth time at a branch that seemed to appear out of nowhere.

"I can, but that doesn't stop my mind from thinking I saw or heard one when I didn't," I replied, sounding snappier than I originally intended.

"Does that mean you don't sense any currently, or you can but they're not that close?"

I stopped, not having thought to check until he spoke. I concentrated, but I didn't think I could sense anything other than my own fears and worries after being on edge for so long. After I informed Ben we were safe, he consulted the map, and we resumed walking, still treading quietly.

"We're almost at the first location marked on here," Ben said a little later. He held up the map and pointed at a small stream that was also marked on it. I'd missed it in the dark, the water gliding along so quietly and smoothly that I hadn't heard it.

We moved closer to it as if it had drawn us and we needed the sustenance it could provide. Neither of us needed water, but we stopped anyway.

All of me wanted to come back during the day when it

was light and I'd be able to see it properly, but even now, the stream held a strange fascination for me. Ben didn't linger, however, and I wasn't going to let him leave me behind.

As he'd promised, we reached the cabin a few minutes later. It was nothing more than a small log cabin that had seen better days. The wood was cracked, and the door hinges were so rusted that the door hung off-center. We would have no trouble entering.

Ben hurried toward the door. When he pulled it open, however, it did nothing but creak loudly and scrape along the small deck in front of it. It revealed an almost empty room. There was furniture inside, but it was old too.

I went in after him, making my hand glow a little brighter to see the interior. A sofa sat on one side, and a kitchen unit with a fridge, stove, and sink on the other. The cord from the fridge ran to a generator on the other side of a second door.

On the right-hand side of the cabin was a bathroom, but I didn't get too close since the smell was less than pleasant. I saw several buckets and no taps, just drainage pipes, giving me the impression that the stream nearby was more than a handy land marker. It was also the water supply for this place.

Most importantly, there was no Anthony.

Ben went over to the cupboards and found they were devoid of food or supplies, but judging by the disturbed dust, just like in the beach hut, this was a recent development.

"He's restocked or eaten here several times," Ben said.

"It's been six days since I last saw him and four since I

found his apartment ransacked. That's quite a few meals to have been out here for."

Ben frowned and nodded.

"He's been alive for all of them if he's eaten his entire stash of food, though," I added a moment later, the thought just occurring to me.

That made Ben's shoulders visibly relax. I wasn't the only one hoping to find Anthony soon and alive. This was an important mission to both of us.

With no sign of him, we had to keep looking. Over by the small table, Ben spread the two maps, and I noticed that the second piece of paper, the one we'd had to reveal, had faded again as if the trick wasn't meant to last.

Once more, Ben and I used our abilities to warm and light it until the map was clear again. It was a strange thing to be able to do, and I marveled that Anthony had thought of so many ways to keep his thoughts safe.

We didn't pause for long, however. The locations marked on the map were arranged in a large, evenly spaced semicircle and looked like a border to something. We would have to try them one by one.

"Where do you think Anthony is most likely to be?" Ben asked.

"Somewhere quiet, up high, and out of the way. Somewhere he can see everything and everyone coming but not feel too exposed," I replied without hesitation, quoting him word for word in something he'd once told me about his apartment and everything wrong and right about it.

I wasn't wrong, but also, it wasn't going to be easy to pinpoint which one of the markings on the map would match the criteria. The marks were nothing more than a graphical representation of where he might be at any one time. We could only look for him and hope.

Ready to go again, Ben looked tempted to take the last of the food. I nodded. With any luck, we'd find Anthony, but if he felt it necessary to have taken food with him, we probably ought to do the same. We were down to a piece of cake each and the dregs of two bottles of water. It made me more aware of how well Anthony must have prepared for this while Ben and I were blundering and needing guides to get us through every part. I was a child compared to my mentor, and Ben wasn't much better. He could do other things, but this...this was Anthony's strong point.

We went back out into the forest, and Ben chose our first targets, three marked places off to one side. The ground sloped up toward them. It was tougher terrain, and the trees were packed in closer, but we kept going and didn't disturb the wildlife too much.

Again, I imagined how beautiful it was during the day, but I hoped we wouldn't still be looking for Anthony then. As we trudged along, I got anxious again, wishing we had more food and that the shadow catchers weren't an almost constant threat in the back of my mind. So far, I'd been chased by the monsters three times and I knew if I came across them again so soon I would wish to be anywhere but here.

It wasn't just what the shadow catchers could do that made me scared. They were creepy and ugly and seemed to have come from the gates of hell.

To my dismay, I was pretty sure I felt the strange, distorted presence of one, but I wouldn't be able to tell exactly where it was until it got close. I reached for Ben and gently took his arm. He stopped, looking back toward me as I dimmed my light, held up a finger, and pointed in the direction the feeling came from.

The worst part was that it wasn't behind us or where we'd come from. It was ahead and off to our left.

We hadn't drawn it here.

That made me more uneasy. It was imperative to move quietly and not draw attention to ourselves. I did not want to be caught by another shadow catcher. Not when we were so close to Anthony, and neither Ben nor I could run for long at this point in our hunt.

We walked on in silence as I monitored the creature, grateful I could feel it and that we had some warning. Knowing it was there also frightened me more than I would have been otherwise, however. My ability was a double-edged sword.

We reached the first of the three markers on the map, a small hide. I almost forgot our protocol entirely and ran to see if Anthony was there. Instead, I controlled myself and walked slowly to it.

The hide was made of sticks and leaves. It was more cleverly constructed than any fort I had made as a kid, and it seemed fairly snug. But it was empty except for a few candy wrappers.

It felt like we were getting closer to Anthony, but I could also feel the shadow catcher getting closer to *us*. This wasn't how I'd wanted this moment to go.

I tried to get Ben to hurry up as we moved to the next hideout, but it was almost impossible to go any faster in the dim light without making noise. I could have brightened the light, but then we'd have been easier to see. We also could have gone faster, but then we would have been easier to hear.

All we could do was carry on as we were and hope it was enough. Anthony had to be out here somewhere.

The next hide proved to be empty as well. I couldn't see that it had been used, but we were going steadily uphill, and I was confident it was where Anthony would have gone.

By the second marker, we'd drawn alongside the monster, and it felt closer than ever. If we moved in this direction much longer, there would be no coming back the same way. We'd have to go forward with a shadow catcher on our tail. It wasn't an exciting thought, but I was tired of running from them.

I focused on finding Anthony since I could do nothing else. Three of us would be better than two, or Anthony's one. With three of us we might be able to figure out how to lose the monster and return to the dragon city again.

As I walked, I wondered why Anthony hadn't told me the truth and taken me to Detaris if he was so worried about my safety. Why had he tried to lead the shadow catchers away when he'd led Ben and me here anyway? No answer came to mind.

An animal shrieked from the direction of the shadow catcher. I shuddered in fear at the sound of the pained animal and halted. Ben encouraged me to continue, and we picked up the pace despite the extra noise. The next hide had to be the right place, or we were going to be in trouble.

Ben spotted it before I did, a box partway up a tree. He pointed up at it before he spotted what I did at the bottom.

An unmoving body at the foot of the tree. I gasped, and my light went out.

I reached for Ben, not sure I wanted to check if it was Anthony or not, knowing it was probably him. We both stepped closer, and Ben's arm went around me. The smell hit us next, and I gagged.

"Come away," he whispered. Neither of us needed to get any closer to know that the worst had happened. Anthony was dead.

My mind reeled as Ben continued to guide me, walking on as if he knew where he was going. How had Anthony died?

I wanted to go back. To shake him awake and get him to explain everything, but he wasn't going to. I knew that too. He would never answer my questions. Or protect me. Or fix anything again.

"Don't cry, Red. Not here. Not yet." Ben spoke more insistently this time, daring to be a little louder, despite the shadow catcher being closer than ever.

I didn't realize tears were flowing down my cheeks until he spoke. He didn't look at me and the words bounced around my head. My indignity at being called Red and not Scarlet vanished when his voice cracked. He wanted to cry too, but we needed to hold it together.

"What if he has something on him we need?" I asked, trying to keep my voice steady.

"We'll come back when it's light."

There was no arguing with Ben's words. But it gave me something to focus on. We had to survive until it was light.

CHAPTER TWENTY-ONE

Time became meaningless, and so did the trees and bushes. Everything was a blur as I focused on putting one foot after the other. With no light to guide us, we stumbled often. When I raised my hand to try to light our way, Ben pushed it down.

I didn't need him to explain why. The shadow catcher was after us, and usually, where there was one, there were several. This wasn't going to be an easy escape. Unlike the previous times when we had been able to get into a vehicle or fly, we were trapped under dense trees, miles from anything.

No sooner had I thought this than I sensed another shadow catcher, the tell-tale uneasy feeling creeping into my mind. I tapped Ben to let him know another adversary was stalking us.

It didn't make sense that Anthony had come here. What had he hoped to achieve by leading them into this forest? Did it make them weaker somehow? They weren't moving as fast, but neither were we. The terrain wasn't ideal for anyone. And why hadn't he turned into a dragon and flown off?

Thinking about the puzzles before us and the challenge of escaping helped me *not* think about what we'd discovered. I didn't want to remember that Anthony was dead. This whole time, I'd assumed he was somewhere else. That he was hiding or kicking ass somewhere I hadn't discovered yet. No part of me had believed him to be dead.

Even now, my heart didn't want to believe it. I didn't want to think about anything but how much further we had to go and if we could find another place to hide. I didn't want to think about never being able to talk to him again.

"There," Ben whispered as he pointed to another box high in a tree. The outline was barely visible in the dark, even though our eyes had adjusted. "We need to get up there and stay up there."

I nodded, hoping this meant the shadow catchers couldn't climb. When we got closer to the tree, I saw there was nothing to aid our climb either. How were we going to get up there?

Without hesitating, Ben's hands shifted, and scales and claws appeared. He looked pained, but he reached forward and dug them into the bark of the tree to climb.

Having no idea how to do the same, I paused at the bottom of the tree and watched him climb. All the while the shadow catchers slithered closer. I felt their presence only a hundred yards or so away. I was in danger of being spotted or sensed.

I looked at my hands, willing them to do what Ben did. Nothing happened but the familiar coldness of fear creeping its way up my spine, trying to override my mind and make me flee.

Halfway up the tree to the box, Ben stopped and looked down. He didn't say anything, but concern came off him in waves when I still didn't follow him. I tried to remember what it had felt like to bash into the building the first time I'd flown, picturing my front claws, but nothing seemed to happen. My hands remained human.

Ben started to come back down, but it was too late for him to help me. The shadow catchers were going to get to me before he did if I didn't start climbing this tree.

Not sure what else to do, I got closer to the trunk and gripped it hard, imagining my claws doing it instead. It didn't help at all, but the shadow catcher stopped, and I heard it sniffing. It had noticed me.

I tried to climb, gripping with my fingers in the rough bark and using the claw holes Ben had made. I also dug in with my feet, but I couldn't get enough purchase.

If I couldn't get up there, I would be dead within a minute. The shadow catcher was only a dozen meters away now.

I closed my eyes and imagined how it must have felt for Anthony to be killed by one of these creatures. It filled me with rage, and before I knew what was happening, I hadn't only turned my hands into dragon claws, but I'd pulled a chunk of bark and the underlying wood off. I flung it so hard at the shadow catcher that it went through it and sort of pinned it to the tree trunk behind it.

It wailed.

"Climb," Ben hissed as another shadow catcher rushed toward me.

I obeyed, and my hands retained their claws as I fought upward. Ben resumed his climb only once I was clear of the shadow catchers.

The first monster had freed itself, and they both circled our tree, hissing and making other strange sounds as Ben and I climbed. It was tough going, and my claws and shoulders started to protest at being used this way. If anything, the pain helped focus me, and I caught up to Ben and passed him on the other side as he floundered, his concentration waning.

The box had a small door. A ladder could be run through it, assuming someone had a long enough ladder. I was closer to it, so I pulled it open. A pile of dead leaves and other debris fell, almost knocking me from the tree before clattering down onto the shadow catchers again.

I couldn't tell if it hurt them, like the first thing I'd thrown. I returned my focus to the box, making sure we could both get inside.

It was even darker inside the wooden structure, and it creaked and groaned when I put my weight on it. I hesitated, not sure how much this thing could handle or if it was even sound enough to hold one of us for long.

There was nothing we could truly do but try our best and hope it held.

I climbed inside. It was a lot darker, thanks to the tiny windows near the tops of the walls.

Ben followed me in, and I gave him a helping hand, although it made the box groan and sway.

"Go back to the other side," he said and gently pushed me away.

It was like the boat all over again. It made a difference,

but I was still worried that the entire floor would give out if we continued to sit here. However, the shadow catchers couldn't get to us. It was a relief to be safe from them.

"Now what?" I whispered after we'd sat there for several minutes, my heart rate slowly decreasing as my body calmed again.

"Now we wait for dawn and hope they give up."

"Dawn won't necessarily help?" I asked.

Ben shook his head, the motion barely visible in the gloom.

As I waited for an explanation, my muscles tensed again and my mind wandered. I had no idea what the shadow catchers needed to survive. Other than seeing them consume water, I knew little. I wasn't sure what was likely to happen and the unknown wasn't pleasant. Ben appeared to be trying to sleep, his head back against the wall of the box and his eyes closed.

Not wanting to disturb him, I tried to copy his actions. If nothing else, it would get us closer to dawn.

Sleep wouldn't come, however. Every time I closed my eyes, I saw Anthony. It was hard to think of him being dead.

The realization that he wasn't coming back and that I would never play board games with him again hit me. Tears flowed down my cheeks, hot and heavy. It was impossible to stop crying, and I didn't try.

It wasn't until Ben handed me a tissue a few minutes later that I realized he had picked up on it. He didn't say anything, but he reached for my hand again.

I took his, grateful I wasn't alone. Anthony had given me someone to keep me from facing these creatures with no aid, but I wasn't the only one hurting. Ben had loved him in another way, and I wanted to comfort him as well.

"Tell me about him," I said, barely above a whisper. Although I wasn't sure it was the right thing to say right now, it was something I'd heard an adult say to another at a funeral, and it seemed fitting now. We would not be able to bury him anytime soon.

"You probably know him as well as I do," Ben replied a moment later. "But there is this one memory that sticks in my head. He used to love the way the rain sounded on the windows in one of the towers. I remember him going out in a torrential downpour to that tower one day to sit and listen. He caught a cold because he got drenched both ways."

I nodded. That sounded like Anthony. More than once, I'd caught him sitting by the window, watching it rain. It hadn't occurred to me that he might be wishing he was somewhere else and remembering what the rain sounded like there. The dragon had given up a lot more than I had realized so that he could protect me.

And it made me wonder why once again.

"What if I *am* an important dragon?" I asked. "What if this is why Anthony was protecting me and why the shadow catchers seem so interested in hunting me down?"

"You're not the right age to be an heir. You're too young."

"What if I'm not?" I asked. "Could there even be a slight chance? A chance that someone lied about my age, or someone could have had me earlier than you think? What if Anthony knew I was the heir?" The words came tumbling out before I could stop them. My cheeks grew hot when I realized I was suggesting that I was a princess. It was every orphan girl's dream.

I expected Ben to laugh, but he didn't respond for a moment.

"I won't deny that would explain Anthony's actions better than a lot of other theories. But..." Ben shook his head. "There would have to be evidence before anyone would even consider it. Many red dragons have tried to claim the throne. Even if it were true, you'd have an uphill battle. It's bad enough being red. You don't want it, Scarlet. You don't need what would come with that."

Although Ben sounded defeated, I heard the honesty in his voice. It was enough to make me not want to be an heir. Whatever I was, Anthony had cared, and he had thought I could achieve something amazing. Even if all I did was help Ben keep going, I had to do something with my life. I was a dragon with powers. I wasn't an ordinary person, and I wasn't an orphan with no real home.

My life would mean more than working in a beach shop day after day.

After that, we waited for the sun to rise. The sky was already lightening.

As the sun came up, I could see the inside of the box, and it looked as weathered as the creaks and groans would indicate. It had holes here and there that weren't part of the design, and it was moldy in places.

I wanted to get out of the hide again, but it had saved our lives, and I didn't want to come face to face with the shadow catchers. Two still prowled nearby, moving back and forth beneath us.

When it grew light enough to see, Ben opened his pack

and pulled out the rest of the food we had. He offered me half.

"Should we save some of this, or do you think they'll give up soon?" I asked.

"Depends if rain is on the way," Ben replied. "If it doesn't rain this morning, they'll be forced to go to the stream. Of course, they could go one at a time, but if it rains…"

I didn't need Ben to say anything else. If he was right, this would go badly. I hadn't looked at the weather forecast recently and I didn't want to, but I remembered the weather report before we'd left Detaris. We weren't due a day of sunshine, and there was a good chance it was going to rain.

While we ate, I tried to think of ways we could distract the creatures, but nothing came to mind. We were stuck, and although we could turn into dragons, we couldn't do it in a box under a dense canopy of trees. Could we fly away from here if we needed to?

"Why don't we just fly away?" I asked Ben a moment later.

"To start with, I'm not leaving Anthony's body."

I'd expected that answer, but he said it with so much passion and a no-argument tone to his voice that told me nothing would change his mind.

"On top of that, we're not supposed to fly in daylight, and we're not going to find it easy to transform in this forest. You might have taken out a few bricks from a building when you were in dragon form, but you had the space. You don't want to transform into a dragon and get a branch in your lungs or leaves in your heart. Trust me."

I got the picture. Turning into a dragon was riskier than it had appeared, and I was grateful that I hadn't known the risks the first few times I'd tried.

"We should sleep and hope this gets better. If we get stuck, we can call for backup." Ben didn't give me any other option but closed his eyes again.

I sighed. I was willing to try, but no sooner had I wriggled to get comfortable than it started to rain.

CHAPTER TWENTY-TWO

With nothing left to drink and the last of the food shared out and eaten long ago, I did not think sleeping or attempting to was the right option anymore.

The morning had come and gone. It had rained several times, although not for very long. We were both wet, cold, and miserable. And to make matters worse, the shadow catchers were more active than ever, and a third was on its way.

"We can't stay here," I said to Ben. "We have to do something. They're not giving up."

Ben frowned and opened his eyes again. I thought he was going to tell me to go back to sleep, but he looked down at the shadow catchers through the gaps in the floor. They were moving around a lot and seemed agitated.

I shifted so I could look at them as well. In the light of day, they didn't look as scary. Their bodies were almost translucent, and the noises they made were less eerie.

They were still very clearly down there, however, and I

didn't know how we were going to get away from them. Not when the rain kept coming and these things fed on it.

"We could probably leap clear of them," Ben said. "Maybe climb this tree, then leap to another and another. Then we'll be on the run. They'll notice eventually, unless we are super quiet while doing that."

It was the first suggestion he'd offered. I was ready to do something, and I couldn't think of anything better.

"We can't stay here. This thing is close to breaking, and we're out of food and water ourselves."

"I bet Anthony left us more clues in this area. He was protecting something, or he came here for something." Ben sounded weary.

"We might have to come back for them," I replied, not sure how much hope I wanted to fan in Ben. "But either way, these shadow catchers want me, or us, and I can't sit here trying to sleep for much longer."

"Okay, but we can't outrun these things for long. We're going to need help." Ben reached into his bag and pulled out the device he'd been handed back in the city.

Although I wasn't aware of exactly what it did, Capricia had indicated that it was important. Once Ben set it off, we were going to have to move again. My stomach tightened, and I tried to remember how I'd turned my hands into claws to climb the tree.

"All right. I'm going to set this off, and then we're going to wait until dark to move. Or dusk, maybe." Despite the "maybe," Ben showed no hint of concern or worry.

"Why are we waiting?" I asked, already sick of this box and hungrier than I'd been in a long time.

"Because if we want to try Anthony's trick, you have to

light yourself up like a Christmas tree. For that we need it to be darker. Also, it makes it harder for them to see us. They do see, just not very well. And I don't know about you, but I'd like to try to sneak past them."

I could hear the exasperation in Ben's voice at having to explain it to me. Waiting would also give the device more time to do whatever it did.

Not sure what else to say, I nodded and sat back. This wasn't the time to be irritating. I needed Ben to survive, and I was going to have to do whatever was needed if we were going to get out of this alive.

My life had been chaotic for the last few days. I would have given anything to have Anthony back and to be cozied up in his apartment playing board games.

Instead, I watched Ben pull open the orb and reveal an orange crystal. A vial of liquid had been tucked under the crystal, and Ben removed it.

"You're not going to like this, and neither are they, so be prepared."

I opened my mouth to ask what he meant, but he acted too fast. He put the crystal into the bottom half of the orb and poured the liquid over it, doing it in a rush, before he could change his mind.

It let out a high-pitched scream so loud I had to cover my ears. The shadow catchers hurled themselves at the tree we were in and let out strange, growling noises.

The tree wobbled and shook, and so did our box, creaking and catching on the trunk it hugged. I hung on and hoped it would subside, but the tree we were in couldn't handle this for long. Ben pointed up. There was no use speaking over such a racket.

Sure that my ears were going to start bleeding or my eardrums were going to break, I watched him turn his hands back into claws and reach up. The box began to disintegrate, and he tore open a section of the roof with his claws and chucked it away, making a large enough gap for us to get out swiftly.

Adding to the destruction he caused, the shadow catchers continued to attack the bottom of the tree. The box started losing planks, dropping them to the ground.

Needing to form claws again, I concentrated, but it didn't work. The noise from the crystal was making my head hurt too much, and I couldn't do anything but cling to what was left of the box.

Ben latched onto the trunk and pulled himself up while encouraging me to do the same. I tried again when the box lost the section I'd been leaning against.

I slid down, clutched at the tree with all my strength, and the bark scratched my exposed skin. The pain helped me focus again, and I managed to get one hand to grow claws so that I could dig into the tree. At the same time, I swung my feet onto another part of the box. More of it fell away.

When one shadow catcher hit the tree, it creaked and groaned and threatened to topple over. As I scrambled higher, the crystal fell, taking the noise with it and allowing me to think a little more clearly.

The orb hit the ground but cushioned the crystal against the fall. The shadow catchers reacted to it as I had, all of them pulling back from the crystal after it landed.

The reprieve allowed me time to think again. I figured out how to transform my other hand, and red scales formed on my fingers along with the claws. It felt strange to see the difference. My dragon abilities would save my life yet again.

I tried to catch up with Ben, but I found it harder to climb than him, and I slipped several times before we were high enough that I could pause. Eventually, I hooked a leg over a branch and rested for a moment.

The tree was still standing, though the shadow catchers were attacking both the crystal and the trunk now. The entire tree shook when the ear-piercing squeal abated. The relief was instant but not complete. It had sounded for long enough that it was weird for it to be gone, and my ears and mind tried to tell me it was still there.

Although the shadow catchers were no longer terrorized by the sound either, they continued to attack the tree, seeming to sense that it put us in danger. It wouldn't be long before the tree gave way, but I tried to climb higher and get out along one of the branches. Ben came around the trunk to join me, and we inched toward another tree.

With each jolt from the shadow catchers, I wanted to whimper. I kept slipping and having to adjust my position. Behind me, Ben fared better, but we were both adding our weight to a branch that was in danger of cracking from our combined weight.

As the branch dipped from our weight, the tree started to crack and splinter. We had no choice but to aim for the next tree and jump.

Terrified of the leap but more scared of the creatures on the ground, I got into the best position. I wobbled with every attempt, and Ben urged me to go out further on the branch we were on.

After another thump from the creatures, the tree gave up, leaning to one side. I clung to our branch, digging my claws deeper, and tried to jump at the same time, resulting in something that only unbalanced me further and left me reeling as the nearest tree came closer. With my claws still stuck deep in the branch, I had nowhere to go.

The top of the tree we were in lodged against another tree. When I was still several feet away, my body was flung toward it by the force of the impact, but my claws refused to budge, holding me fast and straining the muscles all over my body.

After some creaks and groans, we settled and somehow stayed in the canopy. It was nothing short of a miracle that we hadn't been dropped to the forest floor. But I used our good fortune to shuffle toward the next tree.

When I reached the thinner part of the branch, it bowed even more and rasped against another branch of the tree I was aiming for, making enough noise to draw the shadow catchers. I winced and stopped moving. This wasn't going to work if the shadow catchers pinpointed our position. I had to find a better option.

Ben reached out to stop me as I went to inch forward again and pointed down. The shadow catchers had settled now that the tree they'd attacked had fallen and the crystal had shattered. Instead they were milling around like they were looking for something to do.

It was the weirdest thing I'd ever seen.

I stayed where I was. We were safe enough where we were for a while, but I was worried that it wouldn't last. The tree might finally collapse, or the shadow catchers would figure out what was going on and come after us.

As we waited, the sun slipped out of sight, and it got colder and darker. Still, Ben kept his hand over mine to prevent me from moving. Now and then, a gust of wind made the tree sway, but it held fast, and the branch we were on didn't break.

It was an agonizing wait. My body throbbed from holding the position, and my hands shifted between normal appendages and red-scaled claws several times as I fought to stay in the strange halfway house between human and dragon.

With the crystal shattered on the ground, I wanted to ask Ben if it would still bring aid, but I didn't dare speak. Ben didn't either. Neither of us wanted the attention of the creatures below.

I kept thinking of Anthony's body lying exposed and how little we still knew about why he had come here. What had he been trying to achieve? All I knew was that the creatures below had killed him, and now they wanted to do the same to us.

As I thought about my dead mentor, more tears fell. I shuddered as I tried to breathe and cry without making too much noise. Ben shifted slightly, putting an arm around me while we waited. I leaned into him, hoping that we didn't make our perch move after being stable for so long, and then let my emotions out.

It took me a long time to calm down, but Ben didn't let go of me or appear bothered. When I was done, it was almost dark, and we couldn't see the forest floor.

"Time to go," he whispered into my ear.

CHAPTER TWENTY-THREE

In the dark, it was hard to tell if the next tree was in front of us or off to one side, but we needed to get closer and jump for it eventually. I had moved back toward Ben when I'd started crying, but now I was calmer, and it was time to get moving. I inched further down the branch, but it bent alarmingly, and I didn't think it could hold if I didn't jump soon.

I shuffled out as far as I dared and tried to get into a position I could leap from. It was easier than it had been when the shadow catchers had been attacking and getting irate over the powerful wailing crystal.

After working out the best way to hit the tree, I jumped. The branch cracked, and I toppled forward, flailing as I fell.

Reaching out with my clawed hands, I managed to latch onto another branch and swung in an arc toward the next tree. I bumped into the trunk and grabbed on.

Once more, I slipped, but not far, and it only stung a little. I froze when I heard grunts and snorts as the shadow catchers below responded to the new noise. This wasn't going well.

Although I didn't move, Ben did. Instead of joining me, the outline of his body reached into his pocket and pulled something out. With no idea what it was, or what I intended, I waited and watched.

I heard him throw something behind us, narrowly missing our first tree. I couldn't see what he'd chucked, but the monsters rushed in that direction and gave us a clear window. He leaped to the tree I was on and landed above me.

I climbed as quietly as I could. I was terrified, and my whole body ached already, but we were moving again and, for now, undetected.

It didn't take the shadow catchers long to figure out that there was nothing in the other direction, and they slithered back to the tree they had been guarding. I hesitated to move now that I was under scrutiny again, but Ben urged me to keep going and came around the trunk we were clinging to so he could help guide me.

My arms ached as I clung to the tree and climbed higher and higher. This wasn't my idea of a nice way to spend an evening, but I had no choice.

When we reached some thick branches, I climbed onto a V-shaped section of the tree and rested for a moment. It was heaven to take the weight off my arms, and I let them hang by my sides. The climb had turned them to jelly.

Ben found a branch higher up but not too far away and rested as well. When we'd been there long enough that it looked as if the shadow catchers were going to keep guarding our original tree, and no help had arrived, he motioned for me to follow him again.

After a few minutes, he shifted down a large branch away from the shadow catchers and toward another tree. It was hard to keep up with him and stay quiet enough. My body was unable to move with the same practiced ease or grace his did. Although I'd had a physical job and wasn't out of shape, Ben was a level above, and he moved silently.

The night continued to get darker as the evening drew in. This seemed to make Ben happier but he moved so far ahead that I struggled to make him out.

As I caught up, a branch sagged beneath me, although it was thicker than the previous one. Ben was closer to our new destination, and I held my breath as the dragon slung both legs over one side of the branch. He pushed off, then brought his arms up to catch the new trunk.

I held still, but my heart stopped until he grabbed on. Despite my fears, he had made the whole thing look easy.

Not wanting to be left behind and aware of the shadow catchers to contend with, I barely waited for the branch to stop moving before I inched along to catch up.

I tried not to make noise. As I got closer to him, Ben encouraged me on until I was sitting over the side of the branch, legs dangling, secure in the knowledge that he would catch me if this all went wrong.

Not wanting to leave it too long, I leapt. My claws sank into the trunk of the next tree. I slipped when some of the bark sloughed off, and a sticky sap oozed out, getting on my hands. The bark hit the ground at the base of the tree.

Ben put an arm around me and guided me onto a nearby branch as the shadow catchers shifted their focus to us again. None of them looked up, however. Feeling better for actually doing something and putting distance between our enemy and us, we hopped a couple more trees, each time going as far out on a branch as we could before we jumped over to another.

The trees were dense enough, and the branches were sturdy enough at this height that we could have kept going if my body hadn't protested for other reasons.

Nature called. It wouldn't have been easy to relieve myself in the woods at the best of times, but in these circumstances, it was way worse.

Ben motioned for us to return to the ground, and I was more relieved than I'd expected, even with the shadow catchers down there and the knowledge that we would have to go back to Anthony and try to work out what he'd been doing here.

I wanted to run somewhere safe the moment my feet touched the ground, but I let Ben lead the way and set the pace. I wasn't going to screw this up after coming so far.

He took his time, and I focused on moving silently behind him, letting a gap form between us so we could go in separate directions and lead the shadow catchers on a dance to save each other. Maybe one of us could be sure to get to Anthony that way.

Eventually, I reached the bottom and had little choice but to run again out of the safety of the trees. Almost immediately, my hands went back to normal, my mind controlling the partial transformation even when I didn't understand how I was doing it.

Ben put a finger to his lips, and I rolled my eyes, pretty sure that I hadn't intended to make any noise. This was a dangerous situation, and I wanted to get away, not be eaten. Or whatever the creatures would do if they caught us.

The shadow catchers hadn't noticed that we were on the ground yet, but they began sniffing in our direction. It was yet another good reason to get moving. We split up and took care of our immediate needs quietly and in private.

When we rejoined each other, Ben seemed to remember where we'd come from. That allowed me to focus on moving quietly while trying to prepare myself to see Anthony again. The first time, we'd been in such a hurry that I had barely realized he wasn't alive before we'd had to move on.

I was worried about what we'd find when he'd been there in the open for another twenty-four hours. This wasn't what he deserved.

When we got close, Ben slowed. I wondered why when there was a chance the shadow catchers were still after us. I felt them in the back of my mind, still trying to figure out where we'd gone. It wouldn't be long before they found our trail.

When I stepped up beside Ben, I realized why he was hesitating. The smell hit me, and I had to fight not to gag.

"Give yourself a moment to get used to it. Try not to think about it, but we need to find what he was leading us to."

I didn't know how Ben could be so calm. I wanted to ask if he'd seen death like this before and if that was why he knew what to do and how to cope, but it didn't seem like a good question for right now. He was hurting, and I felt the same ache from earlier settle into my chest again. Anthony had been my only family. Sure, I had friends, but Anthony had protected and guided me.

Together, Ben and I stepped forward again, then took another step, our hunters momentarily forgotten. I reached for Ben's hand. Under the dim glow of the moon Anthony didn't look to be at peace, and that hit me harder than anything else. The shadow catchers had killed him. His arms and torso bore the marks of rotted flesh that I'd seen on the guy in the bar several days earlier.

And then nature had finished the job, a swarm of flies buzzing around and maggots crawling in the wounds. Once again, I had to fight not to retch. Ben motioned for me to stay where I was.

"I'm going to need some light, but feel free to look away," Ben whispered as he stepped up to Anthony.

After reaching out my hand in that direction and making it glow, I went to turn away. Seeing Ben reach out for Anthony stopped me. With more tears pouring down my cheeks, I felt a strange sense of fascination come over me. I watched Ben pat Anthony down, then feel in his pockets for whatever secrets they might still hold.

Ben found Anthony's car keys, a folded piece of paper, and his wallet. He took a ring on a chain from around his neck, disturbing the flies.

At the same time I felt the shadow catchers finally catch our scent and move toward us with purpose.

"This isn't enough," Ben said. "There should be another journal if nothing else."

"Maybe we missed something at the cabin," I replied, motioning for him to keep his voice down as I dimmed the light in my hand. "Either way, we need to get moving. They're coming."

He frowned but nodded.

"Climb another tree. I have to check this hide."

I started to argue with him, but I knew I couldn't stop him. We needed answers, needed to know what Anthony had died for. What was so important that he'd led us out here and given his life to keep it from the shadow catchers?

I had no idea, but I couldn't lose Ben too. I ran to his side and concentrated again on forming claws. The danger gave me a rush of adrenaline, and I managed to partially morph again. Each transformation had been different so far, and this one was barely the claws I needed on the ends of my fingers. It would work well enough.

Side by side, we climbed, risking everything just like Anthony had. I refused to think about where I'd land if I fell, focusing instead on the dilapidated box above us and the broken ladder leading to it.

This would not have been a safe option even if we hadn't got flesh-rotting creatures with beaks and serpent tails after us.

When we reached the hide, we could not see a way in. I started to shine a light but hesitated. The shadow catchers were getting closer. My limbs were so tired that I wasn't sure I could hold on for long without sitting on a branch or going into the hide, but after what had happened with the last one, I didn't want to attempt the latter.

In the end, Ben carefully worked his way around the tree, feeling with one hand while holding on with his feet, his knees, and the other hand. It was strange seeing someone move in such a controlled, spider-like fashion and I wasn't sure how he was doing it.

When he'd almost come to the other side of me, he found a small, hinged door on the underside of the hide. He pushed it inward and motioned for me to go first.

I remembered I had light and didn't have to get in without checking it. I heard the shadow catchers slithering, though, and I didn't want to give our position away if they hadn't found us yet. This would have to be done carefully.

Taking a deep breath and focusing on my new skills, I moved toward the door Ben was holding open for me. I put my hand in first and made it glow, then made the area around us darker so no one could see my light.

It seemed to work. Ben gasped. I put my head through the hole to look around. This hide was in as bad a state as the last one, if not worse, and there didn't appear to be anything else inside.

My light wasn't bright enough to see particularly far inside, and there was an area of shadows I couldn't illuminate no matter how I moved my hand. I climbed a little higher, fixed to the tree trunk and trying not to put my weight onto or knock against the wooden hide.

I still couldn't see anything.

With nothing else for it, I climbed inside and did my best to avoid putting weight on the fragile wood. Instead, I moved around the tree trunk in the middle like a strange monkey with one glowing hand.

This place didn't reveal anything new. Whatever Anthony had been trying to draw our attention to, it wasn't in this hide.

Drained and disheartened, and struggling to keep my

body in this strange half-zone between human and dragon, I circled once more. There had to be something.

Three trips around the trunk left me with the same result. Nothing. Not even a scrap of paper. Anthony hadn't left us anything in here if he'd left us anything at all.

We had to move on.

CHAPTER TWENTY-FOUR

When I climbed out of the hide, we had more pressing concerns. The shadow catchers were almost here.

Before they followed us all the way, however, they stopped and sniffed several times, then started to circle. I barely dared to breathe as we watched the creatures move, all three of them hesitating, switching from moving with purpose on our trail to moving around almost aimlessly.

"It's Anthony's body," Ben whispered, bringing his mouth to my ear to do so. "The smell."

In my head, I thanked God for small mercies and relaxed a little. Although we were stuck in a tree and still had shadow catchers on our trail, it helped to know some things made it harder on them. They would keep coming, but it bought us some time.

Wanting to ask Ben what we could do now, but not daring to, I hung where I was and waited. This was less than pleasant, and I was worried that I would fall out of the tree. Ben didn't move either, though his head turned in another direction, studying the dark.

Before he could say anything, I realized I could hear the sounds that had drawn his attention. Someone was moving and talking in the distance. But were they allies or strangers?

We both listened, fear and hope lifting in my chest and making me hurt in a whole new way. Was this the cavalry from Detaris, or were we about to witness two humans walk into their worst nightmare and get killed?

"I'm sure there's a path around here somewhere," a male voice said as a flashlight beam swung back and forth.

It took all my self-control not to yell at them to run. The shadow catchers were beginning to get themselves in order again, and I felt them moving toward the people.

"What can we do?" I asked Ben as the shadow catchers passed us. "We have to warn them or help them."

"Nothing we can do unless we want to expose magic and our nature, and we can't do either of those things. Do you understand?" Although Ben spoke quietly, he placed enough emphasis on the words that I understood I shouldn't defy him. But I couldn't let two people die or be injured without trying to do something to help them.

As the shadow catchers continued toward the still-oblivious pair, I climbed down.

It brought the smell back, but I focused on what I had to do and the words being mumbled as the people tried to find their way in the dark. Ben hissed as if he thought I was being a fool, but he followed me.

When I reached the ground, the shadow catchers were still a fair way off.

Not sure what else to do, I picked up a nearby branch

and threw it at a tree between the creatures and us to get their attention.

It was enough. All three focused on the new noise, but only two of them started in our direction. I'd possibly made everything worse. The shadow catchers had split up and were now chasing both the strangers *and* us.

"Run," Ben said just loud enough to shock me into moving. He pointed in a new direction. I turned that way and sprinted as hard as I could. There was no sense in being quiet anymore. They knew where we were.

I felt two of the shadow catchers spring forward, but the people also yelled something I couldn't make out. It kept the third one focused on them and made me want to make more noise. These people didn't deserve to die because of something I'd brought to the area.

I slowed to see if I could help them, but Ben grabbed my hand and pulled me along.

"There's nothing you can do but bring them more danger at this point," Ben said. "You've screwed up trying to save them."

I wanted to apologize, but it would be hollow. I wasn't sorry, and I wouldn't do anything differently the next time. If there was a next time. Instead, I ran beside Ben and produced a faint light to guide us. I hoped we could find something in the hut to keep them at bay, but when I thought about the events at the bar, I remembered one of the creatures had gone through the door of the building like it wasn't even there.

The cabin wasn't going to save us, and they could slither faster than we could run, especially in a forest. Our only option was to get into the air. We were going to have to fly. And that meant we needed a clearing, not the cabin, and the only place clear enough was near the humans.

I grabbed Ben's hand and tried to tug him in that direction, but he resisted, and we almost fell over.

"What are you trying to do?" he asked when I tugged again.

"Get to clear air to fly. We can morph and fly those two hikers out of here."

"Are you insane? That would break at least three major dragon laws."

"As well as saving our lives and theirs. Surely we're allowed to protect life," I replied, letting go of his hand and heading in that direction.

I didn't get far before Ben grabbed me and pulled me around to face him.

"We're not allowed to interfere if humanity stumbles into danger on their own," Ben said, this time more quietly, as if he wasn't proud of what he'd just said.

"I don't care. I can't let them die, and I'm not dying either." My anger flared, and it made me almost morph where I was. My mind was still telling me exactly where the shadow catchers were and how much danger I was in.

Either Ben was too scared of breaking the rules, or he truly believed they were worth following, because he wrapped an arm around me and tugged me toward the cabin.

Swearing, I fought him, but that only slowed us down, and he was stronger than I was. While we were disagreeing, the monsters closed on us. Once again I almost transformed out of fear.

"Stay human. Trust me, please." Ben tried to encourage me down the hill, and I finally gave in. He had been there since he'd realized who I was to Anthony, and he knew a lot more about the enemy than I did. I was going to have to trust him.

Soon, the cabin was visible. Two more cars were parked in front of it, and people were getting out of them. Ben let go of my hand to wave at the arrivals and got their attention with a shout.

"Two of the typical nasties right behind us. Civilians in the area on top."

I frowned at the vague information. He'd told me there was nothing anyone could do against the creatures, but I ran to them, hoping I might be able to trust in their protection and relax. Ben motioned for me to get into one of the cars, but I couldn't do so at first.

"The civilians have a third after them," I said to the nearest dragon. I recognized him from the city but couldn't think of his name.

"We'd best all move out if there are three of the nasty things," Capricia said. "I'm not tangling with that many. Don't care what the reason is."

"We'll want to come back to collect Anthony's body as soon as we can." Ben kept trying to steer me to a car, but I wouldn't leave. "Come on. Let's get out of here."

"I can't, not until I know everything that matters is safe. Not until those shadow catchers have been dealt with."

A dragon I didn't recognize came over, holding a device that looked like a cross between a gun and a foghorn.

The first shadow catcher slithered into the area by the cabin, and several dragons responded. They shot with this strange device, blowing air, threw rocks and debris, and generally made a nuisance of themselves. The creature barely flinched.

I exhaled and darted to one side, and it flew in my direction. Ben almost tore off my arm as it rushed to one side of me. He continued to try to pull me to safety, but I continued to resist.

The shadow catcher lunged again, and I dodged, pulling away from Ben as I did.

"What are you doing?" he shouted. "We need to run."

"They're after me."

"Which is exactly why you should be running." He tried to grab me again, but I had moved to avoid the shadow catcher. He put himself right in its path.

With no idea what else to do, I made myself as blinding as I could. The shadow catchers screeched as if pained. At the same time all the dragons cursed in surprise.

"Trust a red dragon to freak out," someone yelled from behind me, making me feel even worse.

"You're not helping," Ben said, his voice coming out as a half growl.

This time, I let him pull me away. I whimpered when his fingers dug in so hard that it hurt. He almost wrenched my arm from its socket as he opened a car door and shoved me inside.

I sprawled across the back seat, not sure what he intended to do and feeling scared for a whole new reason. It was an unfamiliar car, but Ben got into the driver's seat and turned the ignition. As he started the car, someone else slipped into the seat beside him.

I pulled myself up. Another person got in beside me, and someone slapped the roof of the car. Ben pulled away, giving me no choice in the matter.

"What were you thinking?" the woman next to me yelled as she strapped in. I rearranged myself since my space was now shared.

I grabbed the oh-shit handle as Ben steered the car around a bend, bumping us over a tree root and narrowly missing the tree's trunk.

"Don't get me wrong. I'm grateful that it worked. You stunned all three shadow catchers, and we got everyone out of there because of it, but I've got two civilians asking questions and seven half-blinded dragons who know better than to use their powers in public. I'm pretty sure that was so bright that satellites picked up on it."

Understanding dawned on me. They were angry I'd used my magic.

"Ben would have died, or me. I lost one dragon who meant the world to me and understood me. I'm not losing the other." I didn't care if they agreed with me or not. It had worked. She'd admitted that.

The trouble was not over, however. As Ben attempted to drive out of the woods the shadow catchers weren't giving up. More of them had arrived, and another darted at the car on the path ahead. It forced Ben to swerve back under the cover of trees.

A strange screech from above caught my attention next. It was followed by the flutter of many wings coming across the top of the car as we reached a small clearing.

"Bats?" the woman beside me asked.

"Yes. The shadow catchers often disturb them and make them erratic," Ben replied. "They're harmless enough."

Despite his assurances, the other two dragons in the car with us seemed to recoil from them, and Ben flinched a few times as they flew at or near the car.

Again the shadow catchers lunged at us, stopping us from heading in a particular direction. The terrain made it difficult to drive fast enough.

"Shit!" Ben was forced to turn again and had to slam the brakes on. The car teetered on the bank of the stream.

"Out, quickly," the woman beside me said, already unbuckling her seatbelt.

I'd not strapped in, but I didn't get out any faster. Fear kept me inside until I'd checked for shadow catchers. They were nearby, but I had a window, and I took it.

As soon as I got out, the shadow catchers detected me. One rushed at me, but someone yelled and startled it. A projectile smacked it in the face. When I tried to duck around it, I slipped on wet leaves. I tried to grab hold of something but went over and splashed into the stream.

I hit the rocks at the bottom, jarring my back and splashing up more cold water. In the sudden chill, unsure where the enemy was, I panicked and fell over several more times as I tried to get to my feet.

Ben grabbed my shoulder and hauled me to my feet. I stopped panicking and took stock of the situation. The other two dragons were trying to fend off the shadow catchers, throwing debris and disrupting the water they were feeding on to buy us time.

It was only working because of the sheer chaos of it,

and it was clear that we couldn't defend this position, especially when the third shadow catcher appeared. The other two dragons backed up until all four of us stood in the stream, and the shadow catchers closed in.

CHAPTER TWENTY-FIVE

None of the dragons appeared to know what to do, and the shadow catchers seemed certain that they had me right where they wanted me.

I could think of only one thing that might help. We needed to morph into dragons and fly away. There was nothing else for it.

I put some distance between myself and everyone else and went to transform.

"Scarlet, no!" Ben yelled. "You can't."

Yet again, he rushed over and grabbed me.

"We can't die here, either." Despite my anger and insistence, the moment was gone. There were too many shadow catchers, and all three of them were rushing nearer.

"Close your eyes." I didn't wait to see if any of them listened to me, and I concentrated on glowing even brighter than I had before.

With my eyes squeezed tightly shut, I only had the

bellows of pain from the shadow catchers let me know my trick had worked.

As soon as I was back to normal, I threw handfuls of debris, leaves, and dirt at the monster closest to us, forcing it back while the creatures tried to regain their vision.

"We should go downstream," I added when Ben realized I was forcing a way out.

"Not unless you promise not to do that again," the woman on my right replied.

"I'll promise to do whatever is needed to save us and the legacy Anthony died for, but I'll only do what is necessary, if that helps."

The woman let out a snort, but she helped me, and we soon drove the shadow catchers back enough that the four of us could run full tilt through the water. The cold made my feet hurt, but I didn't stop. If we ran down the water, the shadow catchers would be forced to travel over it too. With any luck, it would prevent them from catching us.

It wasn't a great plan as far as plans went, but it was all I had. It was clear that the dragons with me didn't have any better ideas.

At first, I worried that it wouldn't work when I saw the shadow catchers join us in the water and gain on us, but we had a good lead, and the creatures were wary of what I was capable of. They didn't get close enough to harm us before we plunged into deeper waters. Within seconds, we were chest-deep and almost had to swim.

Once again water was protecting my companions and me, but the shadow catchers didn't give up this time. They continued to chase us from the banks of the stream, sucking in the water on the edges and following us.

The four of us stuck together, but the creatures were faster than us, and they caught up and drew level with us. There were two on either side now, and my only comfort was that if so many were chasing us, they weren't pursuing anyone else.

I was still worried about what might happen to Anthony's body. No one could go back for him while there were shadow catchers all over these woods, and they couldn't use any magic or fly him out of here. That didn't give us many options.

Through all these thoughts, I kept wading, and the water got colder. I was terrified of what was going to happen if the monsters caught us.

The stream got shallower and slower as the terrain leveled off, the stream widening in this area, and it took the creatures further away from us, giving us a respite. It also made me more aware of the cold now that my soaking wet clothes clung to me above the water line.

It was still dark. I didn't know where we'd end up, but I was leading three other dragons. They must have thought I knew something they didn't about getting away from the monsters. This wasn't the first time I'd managed to avoid them, and every time it had come up in Detaris, everyone had been shocked I'd survived.

Was I capable of something special? If so, what was it? All I'd done both times was use what I had at my disposal. The first time, I'd controlled the light and dark, and the second time, we'd gone out to sea. This time we had sort of done both.

But none of it was working. I'd blinded the creatures twice to keep them from getting too close, and wading down the river was keeping us alive, for which I was grateful. But all this was only buying us time.

We had to save ourselves.

Plenty of solutions came to mind, but they weren't ideal. All of them involved more magic. Ben could warm us up, for starters. We could also find out what the other two dragons could do with their magic. Then we should find a clearing and fly out. That was the simplest way to solve the problem.

At least two of the dragons with us were adamant about not using magic, and Ben had become insistent that I not do so. I understood. Keeping the reality of magic from humans was a noble goal, but it wasn't practical. If the enemy could do whatever they wanted and didn't care what damage they did, we were fighting with a handicap.

"Where are we going?" the woman behind me asked.

"Down the stream until we either get somewhere clear enough we can fly out or they give up," I replied.

"I'm freezing, and no matter what, we can't fly outside of the boundaries of a dragon city."

"Why not? It's pitch black, and I did it only a few days ago."

"Because it's against the rules."

"What happens if you break the rules?" I asked, genuinely curious.

Ben glanced back at me as I asked the question, a warning look on his face, but otherwise nothing for me to go on.

"You get exiled and lose all support from the great dragon race."

"Great. So you're still alive, but you can't go to a place where they enforce the same rules?"

The woman looked like she was going to argue with me but only nodded. Ben looked back at me again as if he wanted to know what I was thinking.

I took a deep breath and continued wading. The stream was getting shallower, and I began to worry the shadow catchers would be able to get to us. This next bit had to be worded carefully.

"If using your magic will save your life, and it's the only way to do so, then it seems that being exiled is the choice to make. Being exiled is better than being dead."

There was nothing but the sound of splashing water as we kept moving. The water was up to our waists, and the monsters started hissing when they realized they were going to be able to catch us.

Not ready to admit defeat, I looked up and saw more sky above us than before. The widening river had created a clearing. We'd have to transform while wading, though, and if leaves could get inside a body, river water could too. Would that kill us? We had to try, however.

"What can you two do?" I asked the other dragons. "Ben can make things hotter or colder, and I can make things lighter or darker. What are your powers?"

"I'm a yellow dragon," one of them answered. She paused as if this was enough information but then went on. "I can play with electricity and do some basic molecular stuff."

"I'm black," my final companion added. "I can provide physical shielding and soften things or harden them depending on what will take a hit better. That sort of thing."

The guards in Detaris had mostly been black, so his latter power made sense, especially the dragons who had caught the learners in my first flying lesson. It was a really useful power for that.

It might not help us now, though. The shadow catchers could make things decay really very quickly. That was the only way I could describe it. Rapid decay.

The memory made me shudder. There wasn't much that could be done to defend against something like that. Physical shields could be as hard as they liked. If they couldn't stop decay entirely, they would be worn out by these monsters. But we had to get out somehow.

"Okay, let's work together. I know we're not supposed to use our magic or fly out of the city, but we need to beat these shadow catchers, and there's no one here to see us as long as we're subtle."

There was no response but Ben stared at me, and the other two dragons stared at him.

"All right," he said after a moment. Both of the women visibly relaxed. Did Ben have authority? Did getting his approval to use magic mean more than I'd realized?

I pushed my questions away and wondered what could hurt these creatures, but no one knew much. I wanted to ask what the survival rate was when a dragon met one of these, but I was starting to get the idea that it wasn't a good thing to know. It did make me wonder how the dragons could know so much about humanity and not know much about their enemy.

I was going to have to discover some way to keep us alive, and I was going to have to do it fast.

The shadow catchers were ahead of us, and I didn't think it would be long before they would come across the front and cut us off. Whatever we were going to do, we had to do it now.

I reached for Ben's hand and the hand of the woman behind me. She reached for the hand of the woman behind her, and we formed a four-person chain.

At the same time the monsters noticed that we were easier targets, and they began a double-pronged pincer movement.

Although we could do little to prevent their attack, I felt a strange sort of calmness. Joining our powers seemed right somehow. Like something Anthony would have suggested.

I didn't know any of that for sure, but I held on tight and waited for the right moment, warning them to close their eyes when I gave the signal.

"Now!" I called. I activated my powers again, not just trying to make me glow brightly but all three of my companions too.

Electricity crackled over my skin and through the water around me, but it didn't hurt me. My skin hardened and warmed as if I was made of something else entirely.

It was an impressive display of power from all four of us, and not only did it repel the shadow catchers by stunning them and almost blinding them, but the electricity acted on the creatures in another way.

The demons shrank back, as if they'd been sapped of

strength. It was over so swiftly I wasn't sure that was what I had seen, but it bought us some time. We hurried down the river, all of us now warmer and braver from the small victory.

A few minutes later, we saw a bridge ahead. On it were several waiting cars with people around them. When he saw it Ben slowed. I didn't know who any of these dragons in human form were, so I let him set the pace and begin to take over. Thankfully, Ben would have appeared to be in charge to anyone on the bridge, not me.

At first, no one saw us coming in the darkness and we waded closer unobserved. Eventually, someone spotted us traipsing closer, and the shadow catchers, who had fallen behind and were struggling to catch up.

There were shouts, then someone started a car engine. They fired at the shadow catchers, slowing them down a small amount with each hit. It was a simple and effective strategy but it required all the dragons to remain at it.

Although I should have felt hopeful, I felt more fear fill my heart and make my feet turn to lead. These were more of the official people from the city. I was likely to be punished for using my powers.

I was left wondering where I would stand when I joined them on the bridge, and they said nothing but pointed toward the cars and the area they were protecting. Was I just going to be in trouble later? Had we got away with how subtle we had been?

With no way to know for sure, I tried to appear as confident as I imagined a red dragon who was an heir should be. Hands still joined, the four of us strode forward to the cars, still wading through the last few hundred yards of river.

I spotted Capricia, the woman who had given Ben the orb. She was coordinating the attack. After conferring with several others on the bridge, she ordered another guard toward danger, the woman carrying a strange shield in her hands. Showing no fear, she got between us and the shadow catchers.

Ben pulled me past her, and the women behind me were so eager to get to the cars that they let go and hurried out of the water. The shadow catchers on the other side tried to cross the river, but one got swept away. The second backed up, screeching.

The two shadow catchers on our side advanced on the guard. She used her power to harden the shield, and the object took on a new sheen, but the demons charged at her.

Without thinking, I ran back to her, dragging Ben with me. He was yet again refusing to let go of my hand.

"Scarlet, what are you thinking?" he yelled. I grabbed the woman's shoulder and activated my powers to add them to hers and funnel them into the shield. At the same time, heat from Ben's magic traveled through me like an electric current.

The shield glowed brightly and beamed light at the shadow catchers. As they crashed into it, the woman braced herself. The glowing shield flared when they hit it, and rebuffed them. The smell of scorching rubber filled the air as the monsters hissed in pain.

They fell back a few meters, swaying and screeching their anger and hurt a little longer.

"Fall back," she yelled.

Ben tugged me backward, and we ran to the waiting cars. The other shadow catcher was heading to the bridge and the road ahead, but the drivers had anticipated the threat and reversed toward us.

Ben dragged me into the back seat of the first car, and the guard got into the front passenger side. She kept her door open slightly, hanging her shield over it and continuing to funnel her powers through it when the shadow catcher on the road spotted me and changed course.

Once again, I grabbed her and Ben and focused my powers. The shield shone even brighter, and I felt the heat coming off it. My body tingled from channeling Ben's power along with my own.

The shadow catcher halted its attack in the face of such a dazzling shield, but the car was moving, and the guard made sure the shield hit the monster with a resounding smack. The squeal that followed made my ears ring.

The hunter became the hunted as it tried to flee. Still shrieking, the creature threw itself into the river. At that, our protector whooped in delight and pulled her shield back into the car, marveling at how pristine it was as our driver took off.

For now, we were safe, but Anthony was still gone, and I still had so many questions.

CHAPTER TWENTY-SIX

The journey was silent and tense for the first few minutes. No one spoke, but everyone glanced at me as if I had grown three heads.

"What?" I asked after a few minutes of this.

"What you did to Leonara's shield... not a lot of dragons can do that." Ben's eyes met the guard's.

"Was that her?" Leonara asked. Our protector finally had a name.

The driver cleared her throat, and everyone stopped talking.

I looked between them all again, getting the idea they weren't saying something and that they were trying to work out what to tell me instead. Eventually, Ben leaned forward and gently placed his hand on the shoulder of the driver.

"I know it's going to be very tempting for you to tell people what happened tonight. How we clashed with shadow catchers and hurt them. But Anthony died in that wood a couple of days ago to protect this secret. To keep

Scarlet from being exposed. None of us knows why, but I know I want to understand more before I tell the world anything."

"Understood," the driver replied. Her voice was familiar, and I caught her gaze in the rearview mirror for a moment. It was Capricia in human form. "If Scarlet is something special, she needs time to figure shit out before there is any pressure on her, or worse."

"Exactly," Leonora said, finally putting her shield down. "This can't be spoken of outside this car. I'm not letting a good dragon die for nothing, even if I want answers as well."

"Then we're all in agreement," Ben replied, though no one had asked me. I opened my mouth to protest, but instead I agreed. If I had done something special that none of the others could do, I didn't want to draw attention to it. I'd acted on instinct and channeled powers I was still learning how to use in response to fear and pressure. I couldn't replicate what I'd done since I didn't know how I had done it.

"What are we going to tell the council?" Capricia asked. "They're going to want a full report. Scarlet activated her powers at several points, and so did others, even if it mostly went unobserved in my case, and the light she created is a normal red dragon ability."

"I saw those light flashes from half a mile away," our shield carrier said, and I winced. I was going to be in trouble when we got back to the city.

"We're going to tell the council as much of the truth as we can." Ben was calm despite the tension in the car. "We were chased by shadow catchers. We escaped down a river after having to abandon one car because Scarlet did some quick thinking and used her abilities, as Anthony taught her, to blind the monsters. We're going to make it clear that we got away without incident after that but that it was close."

"What about the other dragons in the other car?" Capricia asked.

"They'll report what they saw—flashes of light from Scarlet to help buy us time. By that point, she had better control and directed it, and no civilians were at risk of seeing."

Ben's last sentence made me feel better. He wasn't throwing me under the bus or trying to hide so much that the blame could only be pointed at me. I was going to have to mention using magic in proximity to civilians, but I didn't care about that.

I had more important issues, like what else Anthony was hiding for Ben and me and what was happening with his body. I missed my friend, and I also felt as if I had something to find still. Something he'd been trying to tell only me, that no one else had picked up on.

As we continued driving in silence, I didn't feel like I could bring any of it up again. There wasn't a good way to ask about the dead body we'd left behind, and they were all exhausted and had already done a lot.

On top of that, I was also aware that Anthony meant as much, if not more, to Ben than he did to me. I didn't want to remind Ben of the pain of that loss if he wasn't currently thinking of it.

We rode the rest of the way in almost total silence. I dozed on and off until we approached the cliff and drove off it into what appeared to be nothing. When the city appeared ahead of us, there were a lot of lights on for such an early hour.

And when we got closer, I realized the reason. A lot of dragons were waiting in the courtyard in front of the city. Our little adventure hadn't gone unnoticed, and I wasn't sure how I felt about that.

I didn't want to get out when Capricia stopped the car. There were so many people she had to park where she could.

Before I could do anything but stare at the crowds, Ben got out and hurried around to me. He pulled me close when I got out.

"Remember, you didn't do anything but use light magic, and Anthony wasn't hiding anything or leading you anywhere. We just failed to save him."

I exhaled and gave Ben the briefest of nods, and we turned to the men and women approaching us.

"No Anthony?" asked the first elder. She was wearing a gold necklace with interlinked dragons on it.

"Anthony is dead. Shadow catchers had already gotten to him when we found him," I replied, my voice hitching as I spoke. This wasn't going to be an easy conversation.

Over the next few minutes, I and the others in the car were interrogated. We explained as succinctly as we could what had happened. Where I could, I added what I wanted to do about it.

It was a strange story to tell when we were out in the open where anyone could listen, but Capricia, Leonara, Ben, and I did our best. We explained that we had found the body, figured out what had happened, and spent the rest of the night trying to escape the shadow catchers.

I wasn't sure that the elders were interested in something like this, but after we'd told our tale and Ben had made sure they understood that Anthony had been the reason for what had happened, I relaxed. They weren't happy, but they bought our version. Sure, I'd used magic, but since no humans had been present, I wouldn't be in much trouble. That would not be true if they knew the full story.

When we were done with the elders, there were still many dragons standing and waiting. All of them had been there and listening for a long time. Did they care about me? Were they just curious enough to stand out and wait? Why hadn't they left?

I tilted my head to see the two who came forward and greeted me. Flick and Neritas stood side by side, although it didn't look like they were happy about it. They stayed far enough from each other to avoid physical contact, yet they didn't take up extra space in the crowd.

"Looks like you've been through a bunch of shit," Neritas said, his leather jacket billowing out behind him in a gust of wind.

"Yeah, you could say that. Definitely haven't had a good few nights. The last two, especially, were hell. We slept in strange places, we were hounded by shadow catchers, and Ben set off an orb thing that no one seems happy about."

"You used one of the beacons of hope?" Flick asked, his mouth falling open.

"Is that what those infernal ear-bleeding things are called?"

Neritas chuckled as he nodded. "I hear they're noisy. You're drawn to them but also want to claw your brains out."

"That's about right. Thankfully, we only had to listen to it for maybe five minutes. The shadow catchers wouldn't give us any peace while it was going off, and we had to abandon it and let them have at it." I shifted uncomfortably when I noticed more dragons staring at me.

Knowing Neritas and Flick didn't get along with each other, I moved away.

Over the next half hour, I was asked all sorts of questions. I answered them but gave only the agreed information. At some point, Ben joined me and responded to some of the keen dragons. But no one relented until I yawned, and Ben slipped an arm around me to steady my swaying.

"Okay, let's get you to your room and let you sleep in peace and safety," he said loudly enough that everyone else should have heard it.

"Not so fast," someone called from behind Ben. "The elders wish to speak to Scarlet and you regarding the breach of the rules in the chamber."

It was only then that I remembered that Ben had vouched for me, and by using magic when I shouldn't have, I had gotten him into trouble as my legal guardian.

Not that I needed a guardian, but if I had him on my side in the future, it would be useful. Besides, I liked him a lot. He shouldn't be punished for my discretions. I contemplated owning up for what I'd done. I couldn't allow anything else.

"I'll save you a seat at breakfast," Flick said.

"And I'll make sure you get there undisturbed," Neritas

added, making me wonder if the two of them were going to keep trying to impress me so much that they took care of almost everything I did going forward.

I still had a lot to learn, so, for now, I opted to be grateful and leave with Ben once more.

The older dragon put his arm around me and leaned toward me.

"You're doing great so far. This one will be hard, though. They'll know if you're lying. We have to do this by telling the truth in the most economical way."

"How will they know if we're lying?" I asked as he stuck close to me to help me through the crowds. So many people were still here and either trying to talk to us or one of the guards who had helped rescue us. It was overwhelming.

"I don't know. Either an indicator in the room or a psychic bond. I just know it's not worth fighting it."

That didn't bode well for me sneaking around later to figure out what had happened, but that was a matter for another day. I would face the elders if I needed to, and if they didn't like what I'd done, they could go fornicate.

The elders' meeting chamber was at the top of one of the tallest, most irritating towers in the city. That seemed fitting when taken as a whole. It was where I'd have put it. I didn't want people to know my business, and the chamber was well away from prying ears.

As we climbed, I noticed most of the dragons moved out of Ben's way, and in a few cases some even bowed toward him. He seemed to hold a fair amount of authority, so similar to Anthony in some respects that I could have been trailing after my dead mentor. But just as before, I still didn't feel like he could replace Anthony in my life. I missed the patient dragon more than ever.

When we reached the meeting room, I was tired and hungry and it was impacting my mood. It wouldn't have taken much for anyone, elder or not, to get an earful. I wanted to sleep for a day and eat an entire banquet, but I wasn't going to get to do either yet. On top of that, I wasn't sure what was going to happen. This was almost as scary as facing a shadow catcher.

Ben strode alongside me into the chamber, and we stopped in front of a semicircle of almost twenty dragons seated at desks near the opposite wall of the tower. Some desks were covered in books, and others were empty except for a few sheets of paper.

I was also struck by how informally everyone was dressed. This group of people didn't worry about what they were wearing.

"Scarlet, tell us in your own words what happened after you left the city," the older man in the middle requested. He pulled over a nearby pad of paper and lifted his pen.

I told the story that would get me in the least trouble but also sounded believable and normal. I wouldn't have lied if Ben hadn't cautioned me to keep certain things to myself. My mentor had clearly found it necessary. But I didn't want Ben to be in any trouble either.

It was a lot of different criteria to juggle while telling only truthful statements, but Ben filled in the blanks for me and helped when I misspoke. In the end, the story that we told them was about teamwork and dragons finding they were up against impossible odds and doing the best they could.

The elders didn't say anything at first, processing what we'd said. I'd heard no audible indication of a lie detector, and no one had accused me of lying, but that didn't mean they hadn't picked up on something. With a nod from Brenta, they all got up and moved together to confer, acting as if we weren't in the room, but talking with hushed voices so we couldn't hear them.

While we waited for their verdict, Ben once again reached for my hand, taking my fingers in his. I wondered what Anthony would have thought of this. The dragon he'd loved was becoming a sort of father figure, taking care of me as he had.

I'd not warmed to anyone more quickly than I had to Ben. It was as if knowing Anthony had loved him and that Ben was willing to face all sorts of dangers at my side had made it easy to trust him.

My heart would feel bruised, and I would grieve for Anthony over the coming months, but I found some solace in knowing that not only was I not alone, but my old mentor had given me someone to help replace what I'd lost. Anthony had cared enough to not want me to be alone when he was gone.

"It's clear that you have the typical red dragon disregard for rules," the dragon in the center of the room stated after the rest of the elders had returned to their seats and were ready to give their verdict. "It's also clear that you care about your fellow dragons, and you were willing to risk your life, not only to find Anthony but to protect Ben and others around you. You have the courage that is also often lacking in this great city."

I blinked a few times.

"We know we cannot keep you here, and not everyone agrees that you should stay anyway, but I hope Ben, as your legal representative here, will request that you do. You could benefit from honing your skills, learning our ways and our history, and developing an understanding of our way of life."

I considered what he said, taking so long that Ben stepped forward as if he intended to reply for me. I tugged on his hand to stop him.

I wanted to do this.

"Thank you for your invitation. And yes, I will stay, because you're right. I do have a lot to learn still. I also think Anthony would want me to be here. However, I understand enough of your history, your ways, and the life you've chosen to know one thing: you're all cowards. You're afraid of shadows. Afraid of the potential of your own magic. Afraid of humanity and afraid you're going to make the wrong decision.

"Fear never leads to victory."

The elders were stunned into silence, and Ben looked at me as if he couldn't believe what I'd said.

I wasn't done. More thoughts formed in my head and tumbled out of my mouth.

"I will make you a promise. I'll learn, teach, fight, and give everything I'm capable of for the vision Anthony had for me and this great city. Every dragon who gives me a chance will find me an ally they can rely on. Every danger that comes to this city will not find me cowering in some corner but standing against it.

"Also, I'll pour every hot-headed emotion and all my

red-dragon anger into growing and doing what's needed to help the race I find myself belonging to."

"Anthony knew what he was doing, and I think you'll make him proud someday," one elder replied finally, the corner of her mouth twitching up. The others whispered among themselves.

"She's already made him proud, and me too," Ben replied. "If we're done here, elders, I think she's said everything either of us needs to. I'd like to request permission to move her to a room near mine that befits the role she will play in our society."

After a long pause, the first elder nodded.

"As you wish. I think the bravery she displayed this evening has earned her that. You may both go and rest with our blessings."

Ben smiled and motioned for me to lead the way from the chamber. I moved ahead of him to see the first edge of the sun casting its warm light on the dragon city.

This place was my home now, and I had meant every word I'd spoken to the elders. I was going to find a way to protect it from the storm Anthony had seen coming.

EPILOGUE

Taking a deep breath, I paused at the bottom of the hill and looked at the tree ahead, the one with the hide. It was still intact. I wasn't sure what it might contain. Something about it had felt right to draw me back. Ben was with me, but he was finding this part even harder than I was and had hung back.

I slowly walked closer, the image of Anthony lying dead at the bottom of the tree filling my mind. His body had been recovered, we'd held the funeral, and he had been committed to the depths on a boat sent out to sea and set on fire, as was traditional among the dragons of Detaris.

But something had been nagging me for several days. I'd continued trying to translate the journal he'd left, but I hadn't gotten any further. Even more confusing than that, I hadn't found any more copies.

Currently, I had one and Ben had the other, both of us going to great lengths to ensure that they were never together and one was always in a safe place. The book we were using for translation had been copied, and we had taken the original back to the library.

The librarian hadn't been happy when I returned the book that had been washed in the nearby river and dried out again, but I had little choice. I'd needed to take it with me, and I wasn't going to apologize for having to run from shadow catchers and doing what I could to survive.

We were still trying to figure out what Anthony wanted me to do next. After going through the forest cabin again, I had come back to the hides in the daytime to see if he'd been in the process of hiding it somewhere else or if I'd missed something in the dark.

Thankfully, the shadow catchers hadn't been seen since we'd hurt them. Something about having your prey turn around and almost destroy you made a predator warier than before. At least, I assumed that was why they were nowhere to be seen.

Either way, it gave me a clear window to poke around and see if we could pick up the trail Anthony had left for us. I climbed up to the base of the tree as I thought about the dragons in the city and their reactions to me wanting to come out here again.

My few friends were shocked, but they understood. Ben had been almost as eager. The elders had hated the idea, and the protectors of the city had been wary. In the end, it was Ben's decision as my representative. If he said yes and drove, no one could stop me. He had not only agreed but also driven me out here. Although the elders weren't happy about it, they'd let it happen.

I walked slowly around the base of the tree, avoiding stepping on the mark on the ground where Anthony's body had been. It was as if the ground around and under him was cursed by having supported a dead dragon. The grass was less lush, and the flowers were sickly. Whatever had happened, the area remembered it.

But there were no clues.

Not sure what else to do, I climbed the tree, taking my time to morph my hands again. Despite it being a hardwood, my claws went in like it was putty. However, it didn't give as I started to climb.

Red scales appeared on the backs of both hands as my fingers extended and my nails became strong claws I could use to get higher. It wasn't an ideal way to climb, but it worked on trees like this with no low branches to reach. I quickly scaled it, more practiced than I had been the first time.

Looking up to spot the small trap door in the bottom of the hide, I made my way to the right and around the trunk until I got to it. The door proved awkward. Ben had handled them all before now, but I eventually got it open.

I went inside the hide and let the door shut behind me. I was plunged into darkness despite the small window on the other side. I made myself glow, wanting to see the inside as brightly as if it were daytime.

This hide had been one we'd only swiftly checked on the eventful night that we had followed Anthony here. Then the civilians had come, followed by the shadow catchers. Now I had the luxury of time, light, and more knowledge.

Working my way around, I inspected every nook and tiny crevice for anything that might give away what Anthony intended next. I was about to give up, feeling as if

I had tried everything, when I noticed a section of bark that sat at a strange angle. I moved toward it and tried to pull it off.

At first, it didn't want to budge, but then it came away in my hands. Behind it was a small, sealed, opaque plastic bag. A hole had been cut into the wood, of a perfect size to hold it without it showing. It took all my self-restraint not to tear it open right then and there. Instead, I shoved it into a pocket, put the bark back, and climbed down.

I hurried back to Ben, sure he would want to know that we'd found something else, and found him pacing the cabin. Lifting the packet so he'd see it right away, I grinned at his wide-eyed look and explained how I'd gotten it.

"Anthony knew what he was doing, didn't he?" Ben said as he helped me carefully slit the plastic. He waited for me to unfold the paper we found inside. It appeared to be blank again, but we both quickly activated our abilities to reveal some words. We then unwrapped the object nestled in the center of the page.

It was a key. As I lifted it, Ben laughed at the phrase on the paper.

The key to a heart is kept safe by those who value the heart most.

"What's so funny?" I asked, unsure what that meant.

"I gave Anthony this key when we said we'd never part. It unlocks something in my room, and that was what I said when I gave it to him," Ben replied. His eyes were full of tears as he smiled at me.

Without hesitation, I handed him the key and the paper.

"Then it seems you hold our next puzzle piece. Shall we

go find out what Anthony wants us to do to save the world next?"

"Together." Ben took my hand and grinned.

We might not have what we wanted yet, but in that moment, I knew we were going to be okay.

THE STORY CONTINUES

The story continues with book two, *Dragon Seeking*, available at Amazon.

Claim your copy today!

ACKNOWLEDGMENTS

There's always a lot of struggle for me when writing the first book of a new series. Fears that it won't be received very well, that my amazing readers won't like these characters as much, but still the characters talk to me and ask for their story to be told. I have done my best and I will be forever grateful that my readers take the chance on a new book and a new group of dragons or space pirates or fantasy creatures. So thank you readers for being there with every story my fingers type.

And with that in mind I want to thank Bryan. He holds my hand in the dark and reminds me that I don't need bringing into the light but I can be my own light. He listens to me talk about my characters and stories no matter where I'm at and doesn't mind spoilers and although we lost touch for several years in the middle he never stopped believing in me or cheering for me. I wouldn't be writing without his encouragement and support.

To Bear, Andrew and David for helping support me through life, the chaos and also helping me plot the crazy lives in these stories. You guys are my support network in so many ways.

And a huge thank you to everyone at LMBPN, to Lynne and her editing team, to Steve, Kelly, Lindsay, Robin, Grace, Michael, Judith and anyone else I've forgotten who plays a part in getting these books out of my head and into the readers hands. You guys are like family and I'm blessed to have you all in my life.

To my children, for giving me an understanding of what it is to want to be a better example to the people in our world and always having me strive to show you what is possible if you work hard. And for giving me a greater appreciation of what my mother sacrificed to raise me and my brothers. How parents sometimes have to make incredibly difficult choices between what they need and want and what they think their children need. It's not always understood at the time, but I'm grateful for it now.

And to God, because even when the people who are meant to follow you act in judgment and fear of someone different to them, you don't and continue to love and accept everyone, no matter what.

ABOUT THE AUTHOR

Jess is in the process of changing her name. She's been through a difficult year that leaves her wanting a fresh start and a chance to be the person she's always meant to be. Over the next little while all her books will be moving to Talia Beckett and you'll find all future releases under this author name.

Talia was born in the quaint village of Woodbridge in the UK, has spent some of her childhood in the States and now resides near the beautiful Roman city of Bath. She lives with her two tiny humans (one boy and one girl) and near an amazing group of friends who support her career and life choices.

During her still relatively short life Talia has displayed an innate curiosity for learning new things and has therefore studied many subjects, from maths and the sciences, to history and drama. Talia now works full time as a writer and mummy, incorporating many of the subjects she has an interest in within her plots and characters.

When she's not busy with work and keeping her tiny humans alive she can often be found with friends, playing with miniature characters, dice and pieces of paper covered in funny stats and notes about fictional adventures her figures have been on.

You can find out more about the author and her

upcoming projects by joining her on facebook, by watching her live D&D streams, or emailing her via books@jessmountifield.co.uk. Talia loves hearing from a happy fan so please do get in touch!

Talia is also opening up her discord for fans to come chat about what she's up to, and see a few sneak peaks of future work. There's also a chance to become one of her beta readers. If you'd like to check that out you can do so here.

CONNECT WITH THE AUTHOR

Connect with Talia

Mailing list sign up
Facebook group.
Discord group
Actual play D&D stream: Twitch or Youtube
Email address: contact me here.

BOOKS BY JESS MOUNTIFIELD / TALIA BECKETT

Already published

Urban Fantasy

Dragon of Shadow and Air:

Air Bound

Shadow Sworn

Dragon Souled

Earth Bound

Night Sworn

Dryad Souled

Water Bound

Day Sworn

Pegasus Souled

Fire Bound

Light Sworn

Phoenix Souled

Dragon Apparent:

Dragon Missing

Fantasy

Tales of Ethanar:

Wandering to Belong (Tale 1)

Innocent Hearts (Tale 2 & 3)

For Such a Time as This (Tale 4)

A Fire's Sacrifice (Tale 5)

Winter Series:

The Hope of Winter (Tale 6.05)

The Fire of Winter (Tale 6.1)

Guild of the Eternal Flame:

Wayfarer's Sanctuary

Protector's Secret

Healer's Oath

Other Fantasy:

The Initiate (under Holly Lujah)

Writing with Dawn Chapman:

Jessica's Challenge (#5 in the Puatera Online series)

Dahlia's Shadow (#6 in the Puatera Online series)

Lila's Revenge (#7 in the Puatera Online series)

Sci-Fi:

Fringe Colonies:

Alliance

Haven

Rebellion

Rebirth

Reclamation

Star Trail:

Hunted

Sherdan series:

Sherdan's Prophecy

Sherdan's Legacy

Sherdan's Country

Sherdan's Road (A short story in the anthology 'The End of the Road')

The Slave Who'd Never Been Kissed (A short in the charity anthology 'Imaginings')

New Beginnings

Santa's Little Space Pirate

In the multi-author Adamanta series:

Episode 1 – Adamanta

Episode 3 – Excelsior

Episode 8 – Phoenix

Episode 13 – New Contacts

Episode 17 – Sacrifice

Other:

Clues, Claws and Christmas

Non-Fic:

How to Write Lots, and Get Sh*t Done: the Art of Not Being a Flake

<u>Find purchase links here</u>

Coming soon:

Urban Fantasy:

Dragon Apparent:

Dragon Seeking

Dragon Revealed

Dragon Rising

Time of the Dragon (with Andrew Bellingham):

Dragon's Code

Dragon's Inquisition

Dragon's Redemption

Fantasy:

(Tales of Ethanar):

The Pursuit of Winter (#2 in the Winter series, Tale 6.2)

Books under Amelia Price

Mycroft Holmes Adventures:

The Hundred Year Wait

The Unexpected Coincidence

The Invisible Amateur

The Female Charm

The Reluctant Knight

The Ambitious Orphan

The Unconventional Honeymoon Gift

The Family Reunion

The Immortal Problem

The Unremarkable Assistant

Coming soon:

Mycroft 11

OTHER BOOKS FROM LMBPN
PUBLISHING

Sign up for the LMBPN email list to be notified of new releases and special deals!

https://lmbpn.com/email/

For a complete list of books by LMBPN please visit:

https://lmbpn.com/books-by-lmbpn-publishing/

www.ingramcontent.com/pod-product-compliance
Lightning Source LLC
LaVergne TN
LVHW041754060526
838201LV00046B/996